His Darling

Friend

A Touches of Austen Novella

LEENIE BROWN

LEENIE B BOOKS
HALIFAX

His Darling Friend

Contents

Dear Reader,

This novella is part of my *Touches of Austen* Collection of Austenesque stories. These stories feature original characters and plots that have been touched in some way by the influence of Jane Austen and her novels. The story you hold in your hand, *His Darling Friend*, has elements in it that harken back to *Emma*.

To help you on your way in seeing the influence of Jane Austen's writing on this novella, I will tell you two of the items that pay homage to the original work.

First, we have two long-time friends and neighbours as our hero and heroine. However, Mr. Shelton is no Mr. Knightley, and Miss Hamilton is no Emma. In fact, Miss Hamilton is more like Mr. Knightley, and Mr. Shelton, being a rakish sort of fellow, is not exactly an Emma even if he is the one thinking he can matchmake and who often gets scolded.

Secondly, there is the title of the book. In *Emma* when Mr. Knightley is proposing, he calls Emma his dearest and most beloved. In this story, Mr. Shelton calls Miss Hamilton something similar — his dearest, darling friend. And that is where the title comes from.

There are other nods to Austen in this story — some were purposefully done, others just serendipitously happened. Which ones will you notice? Will you see any traces of Mrs. Weston or perhaps even someone akin to Mr. Elton?

If you would like to share your observations about which elements you thought were Austen-inspired, you can do that in my *Touches of Austen Readers Group* on Facebook.

Happy Reading!

Chapter 1

Roger Shelton slumped down on the cream-coloured settee in the far corner of the Abernathy's drawing room next to a pretty young lady whom he knew would not bat her lashes at him or smile coyly as all the other eager young women at this house party seemed wont to do. Not that he blamed them, of course. He would make a fine catch if he were ready to be caught.

"Why must we attend these things?" The petite blonde next to him whispered.

"Because neither you nor I are married, and our parents wish to be rid of us," Roger replied.

How often had he heard his mother bemoaning his unmarried state to her mother, who would return her own tale of woe about having an unwed daughter? It seemed to be a frequent bent in nearly every conversation when their two families gathered for tea, dinner, or whatever excuse either her mother or his could conjure for themselves to be together.

"Perhaps your mother would like to see someone take over your care, but my father is not anxious to send me packing," his companion retorted.

Roger chuckled. He enjoyed these moments of unfettered banter with his friend. She would speak openly to him, for she wanted nothing from him. Not a kiss, not a dance, not a marriage – with her, he was free to be himself. Even if that often led to her scolding him.

"Is that so, Vic? Then why do you suppose your father gave me this." He withdrew a small packet from his pocket and handed it to her. "I was to deliver it to you here with the accompanying message that he trusts your decisions but would like to meet the chap before the vows are read."

With a resounding thump, Victoria Hamilton's right hand connected with Roger's chest, causing him to exhale quickly. She was not one to pull her punches as some chits might. She did not care one jot if Roger thought her less than delicate, and he liked that about her.

"He said nothing of the sort. You are the worst

liar – no! I cannot say that. I know you to be a very good liar – but in this, you shall not deceive me."

"It was worth a try," Roger admitted, rubbing the slightly sore spot on his chest where she had hit him.

He had known she would not believe him. Her father was too kind to tease in such a fashion, and he was in no rush to see his darling daughter given away to anyone.

"Your father did give me that package for you. That is the truth. As is the fact that my mother suggested I take a good turn through the ladies of the room looking for more than pleasant curves and a willing smile."

"You are dreadful!"

Roger placed a hand on his heart. "I promise you she said that very thing. Mother is not known for her delicacy when chiding me." In that way, Victoria was a lot like his mother. "There was also something in her diatribe about grandchildren before she turned her toes up." He shot a devilish grin at his friend.

"Do not say it," Victoria hissed.

It amused him how her expression was appropriately appalled at the mere thought of what he was about to say. She did know him well. Of course, her expression would not prevent him from continuing.

"Mother was not pleased when I suggested that producing children did not require a marriage license."

"You did not!" Victoria shook her head. "Of course, you did. I can nearly hear you saying it."

"I am wounded."

"By the truth?"

"No, by the thought that you think I would –" A severe glare stopped his words.

"Are you or are you not, Roger Shelton, the charmer of ladies, the stealer of kisses, the seeker of pleasure?"

He could not refute her statement, so he did not. He simply sat quietly and waited for her to continue.

"None of that embarrasses you as it should," she muttered. "Did you get your hunter?"

Apparently, the discussion of his ill behaviour was at an end.

He nodded and extended his feet out in front of him, crossing them at the ankles and making himself very comfortable. "Clayton helped me."

"Mr. Clayton?" she asked with a smile that caused him to raise a brow in question. "He is pleasant," she retorted with a huff. "Naught else."

"That is good to know since I do believe he is getting married. At least he seemed on the point of proposing when I left Stratsbury Park, and I dare say the lady was only waiting for him to ask. She'll accept him, happily."

"Indeed?" Her tone was filled with delight.

"Thanks to my assistance."

Victoria blinked, and her mouth dropped open for a moment. "I beg your pardon?" she asked incredulously.

Was it so impossible to believe that he would help a friend in such a way? He supposed it likely was. He was not known as the sort of gentleman who looked for ways to be snared. But then, he was setting the parson's trap for his friend and not himself, so it really should be more believable.

"I may have pointed out to Clayton how he and his neighbour Miss Tierney would suit each other quite well."

"You?" There was not a single ounce of belief in her tone. "You helped a fellow charmer make a match?"

Ah, that was why she was so disbelieving. It was not just any gent he had helped. Graeme Clayton was nearly as much a rogue as he himself was. Roger shrugged and puffed out his chest a bit. "I have always been very good at reading people."

She shook her head.

Why did she have such a difficult time believing that he could do anything good?

"I assure you I am. How else have I remained a bachelor for so long when there are so many who would trip over each other to be my bride." He winked at her, and she rolled her eyes, just as he knew she would.

"I am certain I could find a match within the assembled hopefuls. Not for myself," he clarified. "I am not in any hurry to be married, but several gents seem eager and, yourself excepted, there is not a lady here who is not hoping to snare a husband."

"I am not the only lady who does not feel a need to rush to the altar," Victoria retorted as if he had affronted her most grievously, but there was a small curl of her lips that told him she was not entirely put out with him.

He leaned toward her. "Marrying at three and

twenty would not be rushing," he muttered near her ear.

"Oh, good heavens, you have been talking to my mother, have you not?"

Roger nodded. "Why do you not marry?"

"Why should I?"

"Do you really wish to live with your brother and his wife?"

Victoria expelled a great sigh but said nothing. Roger knew very well that Victoria did not like the new Mrs. Hamilton and had been quite delighted to hear that her brother and his new wife would be spending a great deal of time in town or at a rented cottage near the sea when the weather got too warm to abide London.

"Why do you not marry?" she asked instead of answering his question.

"I do not marry for quite noble reasons, or so Miss Tierney says."

The brow over her left eye rose skeptically. "And what pray tell are your noble reasons?"

Roger folded his arms and looked at her — his dear friend who did not believe there was a noble bone in his body. "Do you not think me capable of being honourable?"

Her lips pursed, and her brow furrowed. "It is not that you are incapable of such," she said after a full minute of silence. "You know that I have always told you how honourable you could be. You have the potential to be a very fine gentleman who is sought after for more than his looks and a bit of fun."

Her cheeks coloured slightly as she said those last words. Impropriety of the sexual nature always made Victoria blush when she referenced it. She was as proper as he was improper. She might not agree with all of society's strictures, but her behavior was always impeccable. She assured him that it was possible to both disagree and still adhere to the rules. He was not certain he believed her.

"If you think me capable of being honourable, then why do you question so vehemently as to whether or not my reasons are noble?"

She expelled an exasperated huff. "Because I see little evidence of your nobility when it comes to the fairer sex." The blush on her cheeks deepened a shade. "And I did not question you vehemently. I questioned. That is all."

Roger's lips tipped up on one side. "I will only

tell you my reasons after you have told me your reasons for not marrying."

Her eyes grew wide, and she shook her head. "I cannot."

"Cannot or will not?"

"Will not."

That answer stopped Roger from any further prodding. They had not had any secrets – or at least not many secrets – ever. They had shared nearly everything with one another growing up, and it bothered him that she would choose now to decide she would keep something so interesting from him.

"I would not tease you," he offered.

"I know you would not, but..." She sighed and shook her head. "I would feel too foolish."

She did not trust him. She said she thought him capable of nobility, and yet, she did not actually trust him. It stung as much as if she had slapped him. He drew a breath and released it.

"Very well," he said, "then, I shall not tell you mine. You may write to Miss Tierney to discover them if you wish, but I shall not tell you."

"I have hurt you," she said softly as she placed a hand on his still folded arms.

Feeling very much like a petulant child, he

merely shrugged and changed the subject – somewhat.

"Who shall we see matched?" He would prove to her in some way that he was capable of thinking about marriage in a serious fashion.

"I really could not say," she replied. Her brow was furrowed. "Are you well? I did not mean to – "

"Perfectly," he cut off her apology. He did not wish to hear it at present. "I am perfectly well."

He was not. His closest friend in all the world had just told him in so many words that she did not trust him. However, he was not about to admit to it.

"I say we spend a day considering who might complement whom at this gathering, and then I shall begin." He leaned close to her and nudged her shoulder with his. "If you would be so kind, I should rather appreciate it if you would attempt to discover which sort of gentleman we might match with Miss Grace Love."

"Why?"

There was that skepticism again.

"She knows my reasons for not wishing to marry since we played a little game when I was visiting Clayton, and rather than heeding the fact that I have no desire to marry, she has taken it upon herself to follow me around and attempt to prove my reasons are not insurmountable." He lowered his voice. "Frankly, I do not trust her. She is very marriage minded and only seventeen." He shuddered.

"Far too young to be attached to an old man such as yourself?"

"Far too flighty. And I am not old. Might I remind you that you are only four years younger than me?"

"Younger is the important word," Victoria said with a laugh that always lifted his spirits — even when he was put out with her. "I shall see what I can learn about Miss Love."

"Thank you." Roger pulled a second small package from his pocket and after rising handed it to her.

"What is this?" She turned the item over in her hands.

He smiled. "Did you really think, my darling friend, that I would not remember your birthday as I always have?" He winked and then giving her a bow, left her so that she could open his gift in private.

Chapter 2

Victoria should have known Roger would not forget her birthday even if she were not at home. He never had. Not once in all the years she had known him, whether he was at home, school, or elsewhere, had he ever forgotten. No matter where he was, there would always be a gift for her on her birthday.

She knew what would be inside the package even before she untied the lavender ribbon that held it closed. The colour of the ribbon never changed because, while her friend might be a charming rake who sported a devil-may-care façade, he had a secret sentimental side to him, and he knew that lavender was her favourite colour.

Victoria wound the ribbon around her finger and, then slipping it off in a neat little bundle, she put it in her pocket. She would incorporate it into something she wore later. She always did, and Roger would always try to guess how she had used it. It was part of the tradition which never changed, just as what was inside was also unchanging.

Girls like flowers and pretty things like butterflies. That was what Roger had said the first time he had presented her with a birthday gift when she was eight and he was twelve. His sketches had improved since then.

She lifted the carefully cut pasteboard card from its wrapping. This year's gift was designed as a calling card might be. On the left-hand side of the card, there was a delicate daisy with it's petals drooping down and slightly damaged, and a butterfly, perched on the center with its wings folded, and then on the right, in eloquent writing with several swoops and swirls, in place of her name, it bore the words: "My Dearest, Darling Friend."

Roger Shelton was a trial at times, but then, at moments like this, she remembered just why she loved him as she did. A more loyal friend could not be found. He bore her scolds with great aplomb and seemingly sought out such lectures, for why else would he share some of his exploits with her?

She scanned the room. There he was, watching

her from across the drawing room where he was just entering into a conversation with some gentlemen. She smiled at him and pressed the card to her heart. His replying look of pleasure was perhaps the best part of his gift. She sighed. He had such potential to be a much-sought-after gentleman – and not as he was now, but for proper reasons.

"What is that, Miss Hamilton?" Miss Grace Love, the very person Victoria was to seek out, plopped down on the settee.

"A birthday gift from a good friend," Victoria replied, tucking the card away before it could be examined by the young lady next to her.

"From Mr. Shelton?"

There was perhaps too much curiosity in the young lady's tone. Miss Grace almost sounded a trifle jealous.

"Yes," Victoria replied. "We are neighbours, and our parents are great friends. He brought me a few things from my father as well."

"You are friends of long standing then?"

Victoria nodded. Her companion's tone had shifted from one of jealousy to hopefulness.

"He had said, when we were at Heathcote

together – that is my cousin's home — that he was not going to attend this party."

"He does try to avoid gatherings like this," Victoria assured her.

It was rather unusual to see Roger in a setting such as the Abernathy's House Party. He preferred soirees with gardens, alcoves, and a few less-observant chaperones. Soirees were events where one might glide in a few moments late and leave as early as was needed. However, at a house party, all gliding in and sneaking out was taken note of, and should any young lady and young gentleman be absent at the same time, rumors of compromises and wedding were sure to race ahead of the young couple's return to the room.

"It is pleasant to see him," Miss Grace said.

If words could be sighed, Miss Grace's pleasure at Roger's presence had been, and Victoria could see why Roger was hoping to rid himself of the young woman's attentions. Grace oozed what Roger would call the toxic fumes of the death of a bachelor, who would most likely not go to his final resting place, meaning his marriage chamber, willingly. Victoria felt her cheeks heat at her thoughts. He was shocking even when he was not present.

"I was surprised by his arrival." She looked at her companion. "He is not here to find a wife."

"Oh, I know," Grace assured her. "But he might change his mind."

"I very much doubt it. There is no delicate way to say this, but I would have you be warned. Mr. Shelton's reputation is not... well... it is not good. He is a charmer, who is looking for some fun and not a wife. He will flirt, but he will not offer marriage."

"Do you wish to marry him?"

Victoria blinked. That was a very forward question. "I... I... I do not have any intention of marrying just yet."

"You do not?" The question was accompanied by a look of utter horror. "But do you not fear being thought of as on the shelf?"

"Not yet." In a year or two that might become a concern.

The young woman next to Victoria gave her a perplexed look as if such a thing were too difficult to comprehend.

"I should very much like to marry," Grace said with some feeling.

That was not a great revelation to Victoria, but

it was a good opening to discover information she could use to keep Roger unfettered. "You are so young. Why would you wish to marry so soon?"

Grace pulled her lower lip between her teeth and leaned closer to Victoria, lowering her voice to a whisper when she spoke. "Well, you see, my sister is soon to be married so remaining at home would be dreadfully dull without her."

"Is that the only reason?" It was not a very good one in Victoria's opinion.

"No, I also love children and should find great pleasure in decorating my own home without my sister telling me how it should be done."

Decorating one's home and being rid of one's sibling were also not good reasons to marry. A house could only be decorated so many times, and siblings? Well...

"In my experience," Victoria said, "older sisters will still tell you how things should be done even after both they and you are married. I have seen it."

"Felicity will be too busy with her parsonage," Grace assured Victoria.

"That is happy for her then."

"And me," Grace added.

"Quite so," Victoria agreed. No matter how

much she wished to dissuade the young woman of her ill-thought-out notions, it was not Victoria's job to do so — if it was even possible. Her task was to discover what sort of gentleman Miss Grace Love might consider for a husband.

"Aside from my friend, who has just arrived, have any of the other gentlemen caught your eye? You need not worry about telling me, for I assure you that I am only here because my mother requires me to be. I will not try to steal any of the gentlemen here away from you."

"Oh!" Grace blew out a breath as if something of great importance and effort had been asked of her. She obviously took the duty of finding and securing a husband quite seriously.

"Let me see." Once again, she drew her bottom lip between her teeth as she studied the gentlemen in the room. "Mr. Ainsley has very nice eyes. They crinkle when he smiles as if he feels the expression throughout his whole being. It is good to find a man who can feel so deeply, do you not agree?"

Victoria nodded. "A feeling husband is a good thing. I should like someone who could commiserate with me on things."

"Mr. Ramsey is..." She sighed.

"He does cut a fine figure," Victoria agreed.

"And so tall."

"That he is," Victoria agreed. Mr. Ramsey was likely the tallest and broadest gentleman in attendance. "A lady would feel well protected with him by her side."

"Oh, she would."

Victoria pressed her lips together at the near desperation in Grace's tone. "What of status and fortune? Do you prefer a title? Or do you wish for an estate in a particular location or of a certain size? Would a home in town be desired?"

"I had not thought about the size of a man's estate, although I had thought a home in town, even if just rented for the season would be quite nice."

"If you enjoy the season, that is a must. But what of a title?"

Grace shrugged. "A title would be nice, but truthfully, it is not necessary. As long as he has a sufficient income to be comfortable – even after children are born."

"One must not forget about the children or their education," Victoria agreed.

"Yes, yes, their education must be the best. My

parents spared no expense on mine or my sister's education. We are both very accomplished." Victoria's companion lifted her chin as she said the last part.

"Then you will wish for a gentleman who values such things."

"Without a doubt, but what gentleman would not?"

Victoria grimaced. "Mr. Shelton," she whispered. "He is much more of the philosophy that education can be found in play and leisure. His children would, of course, have a governess or tutor, but he is not favourably disposed to sending them away." She shrugged. "I believe he did not enjoy his own schooling and thinks it can be accomplished in a better fashion than what he experienced."

"Indeed? Well, that is most shocking!"

"I agree." It was a lie. Victoria liked the idea of being able to instruct her daughters, should she be so blessed as to have any, in a great variety of subjects – even those not considered useful to the female mind. "However, since you are so accomplished, you might do well in such a situation. I am certain you could teach your children many things – music, art, language, reading, and so forth."

"Me? Teach my children?" Grace's lashes fluttered. "I had not considered I should have to do that."

"You would find it unpleasant then?"

"Intensely." She sighed. "But Mr. Shelton is so perfect."

"Dashing, wealthy, a good conversationalist, and even an excellent dancer," Victoria said in support of Grace's statement. "But then there is also his penchant for pleasure which could cause an issue."

"Oh, no! He has said it will not."

Victoria's brow furrowed. "He has said what?"

Grace scooted closer to Victoria and turned her head to look directly at her companion. Then, in a low whisper, spoken in such a fashion that her lips moved very little, she said, "He thinks he is not ready to marry because he knows that when he does, he will have to give up his freedom since being a husband comes with great responsibility. He does not take such things lightly."

"He said that?"

Grace's head bobbed up and down.

Victoria looked across the room to where Roger

was deep in conversation. He considered marriage so seriously? There still was no evidence of such a thing.

She shifted and the corner of the card in her pocket poked her leg and her conscience. Roger treated friendship with great respect. It would stand to reason that he would also treat a wife in the same fashion. He taunted his mother – and hers – but he was always true to his word to them both. No wonder he had sounded so hurt earlier.

"There is still the matter, however, of educating your children, and that is a difficult thing to overlook. So, what if you and I attempt to discover what Mr. Ramsey and Mr. Ainsley think on that subject?"

"You would assist me?"

"I would." Victoria would do anything to keep her friend from an unhappy match, even if it meant assisting this young woman in finding a husband.

"That is so generous of you. My mother is excessively busy with Felicity. We expect there to be a happy announcement from that front in the near future, so I dare not pull Mama away from such a thing. But..."

"You would also like your chance at happiness?"

Grace nodded vigorously. "I would like that so very much."

"Well, then," Victoria said, rising and extending a hand to her young companion, "shall we take a turn around the room and see if we can discover some happiness?"

Chapter 3

Roger skirted the edge of the room. Their host had announced that there would be an impromptu musical exhibition in two hours time, and since he had no desire to be pressed into singing or some such thing, Roger was making his escape as quickly as he could.

"Mr. Shelton, do you sing?" Miss Grace stepped into his path.

"He does not like to sing in public." Victoria's look was apologetic.

She had likely attempted to keep Miss Grace from approaching him with her plan to conscribe him to a musical display.

"But it would be so delightful to have him sing while I played."

Could the young woman look any more forlorn without actually pouting? Roger did not like sulking misses. He did not like flighty, fidgety misses. He did not like misses who clung to a fellow or followed him around without invitation. There were a great number of misses he did not like, and house parties seemed to be where they gathered to perfect their evils. Due to the attentions of several hopeful misses, the afternoon had been trying to say the least. He was only staying for a few days to humor his mother. Then, he would sneak off to some friend's home which was free from females seeking to snare him.

"I have never sung with anyone playing except for when required to do so for my and Miss Hamilton's parents."

Victoria's eyes narrowed just as Grace chirped with delight. "Then, perhaps Miss Hamilton could play, and you and I could sing."

"No," he said at the same time as Victoria.

"I do not sing duets," he continued.

"And I do not wish to perform. I hope to only enjoy the music," Victoria added.

Roger would be sorry to not hear his friend sing or play. She was not without a good bit of talent. However, he also understood her desire to not be paraded in front of all the gentlemen here as if she were actually interested in marrying one of them. She was not. She had said so.

"Did I hear talk of a duet?" Mrs. Abernathy had turned from the direction in which she was headed to join Roger's unfortunate group.

"No," Roger answered while Grace said "yes."

Mrs. Abernathy laughed. "It cannot be both yes and no. It would be excellent to hear some gentlemen lending their voices to our production." She held up a hand as Roger opened his mouth to refuse to sing once again. Her other hand waved a set of gentlemen towards her.

Much to Roger's dismay, the three gentlemen obediently responded by joining them.

"I have had the notion that some duets would be just the thing for our musicale. I am certain there is at least one or two of you gentlemen who would be willing to assist me in this," Mrs. Abernathy said.

The suggestion was met with silence and an eagerly expectant look on Grace's face.

"My Amelia is playing the harp, of course. However, she can also play the piano very well, and I am certain it would not tax her too much to prepare two numbers." The lady smiled and straightened the cuff of her sleeve. "She is very accomplished."

There was a lilt to her voice that suggested the gentlemen gathered around her should consider her daughter as an excellent choice for a wife – because she could play more than one instrument, which was ridiculous in Roger's way of thinking.

His left eyebrow rose as he shared an amused look with Victoria. How often had they discussed what he considered an accomplished wife to be? Not once in all of those discussions had the necessity of playing both the piano and harp arisen as requirements for Mrs. Shelton.

"Miss Hamilton and Miss Grace could play for two of you and..." her eyes searched the room. "I am certain we could find someone to pair with the remaining gentleman."

"I am not playing," Victoria said softly. "I am certain my skills are not prepared to be put on display with such short notice. I am dreadful about practising, you see." Her cheeks flushed, and she glanced uneasily at the gentlemen of the group who were not Roger.

Roger's brow furrowed. Why would she care what those gentlemen thought of her lack of practice? Had she set her cap at one of them? The thought caused his scowl to deepen, though he knew it could not be true. She had declared she was not ready to marry.

"I am certain you must have one song that is familiar enough to play," Mr. Carlyle said with a smile.

"I am afraid I do not," Victoria replied, returning his smile.

"A simple piece could be practised with time to spare," Mr. Carlyle pressed much to Roger's annoyance.

Victoria had said she did not wish to play. Why could it not be left at that? Why must this... this... popinjay attempt to persuade her to do what she did not wish to do? He folded his arms and glared at Carlyle.

"What of Miss Grace," he said. "She was eager a moment ago to have someone sing with her."

Carlyle shrugged and looked to his friends.

The rude dolt! That man was not good enough for Grace – for whom Roger only cared a trifle –, and a far cry from even touching the edges of good enough for Victoria. Carlyle was one gentleman at whom Victoria would not set her cap if Roger had anything to say about it – which he would make certain he did.

"How about you Mr. Ainsley?" Victoria asked.

Roger stopped glaring at Carlyle long enough to notice a speaking look pass between Grace and Victoria. Mr. Ainsley, was it? He had seen the two ladies conversing with several young bucks during the past hour and a half. One of them had been Ainsley.

The eyebrows on the gentleman being questioned flew upwards as his eyes grew wide. "I am not opposed to singing."

"Will you sing with Miss Grace playing?" Roger asked.

The gentleman looked as if he wanted to loosen his cravat. Poor fellow to be put upon as he was being. Not that Roger felt too much pity for him, for the removal of Grace and the probable match that could be made was worth the gentleman's unease.

"Yes, yes, of course," Mr. Ainsley muttered.

"Excellent!" Mrs. Abernathy cried. "That is one duet arranged. Now, about Mr. Carlyle, Miss Hamilton."

Oh, for heaven's sake! Did no one understand the words *I am not playing*?

"I am sorry," Victoria said with a small shake of her head.

"Then, perhaps my Amelia would suit, Mr. Carlyle?"

The man did not look as if he wished to be suited by anyone, save Victoria. He gave Victoria one more pleading look.

"I will see what I can find," Victoria said.

She was going to play for the fool? Roger snapped his mouth shut.

"Then there is only Mr. Shelton and Mr. Walcott who need accompanists."

"No, it is just Mr. Walcott," Roger inserted. "And if he were to sing while Miss Abernathy played, all your troubles would be at an end."

The lady before him gave him a cajoling look. "Mr. Shelton, you simply must sing. I can tell you must be very good at it for when you speak there is such a melodious quality to your voice."

"No," Roger said. "I have already told Miss Grace that I have only ever sung with Miss Hamilton playing, and since she is already playing for Mr. Carlyle and requires time to practice for that performance, you will just have to do without me. However, I promise to applaud loudly for Miss

Grace, Miss Hamilton, and, of course, your daughter. It will be a great pleasure to partake in listening to all the musical selections." He bowed and made to leave them.

"Then, Miss Hamilton simply must play for you, and I shall find another lady to assist Mr. Carlyle."

Roger shook his head. "Oh, no, Madame. I could not do such a thing to Mr. Carlyle. He worked so hard to acquire Miss Hamilton. It would be a grave injustice to snatch his prize from him." Even if it would make Roger feel quite happy to cause the gentleman some discomfort after the way he mulishly pursued Victoria. "On this, I will not be moved," he added to his host.

Mrs. Abernathy scowled, but only for a moment. Then, her ever-pleasant smile – the same unflappable smile every good hostess wore – found its way back onto her face.

"I shall clap the loudest," Roger assured her.

"Wait," Victoria said before he could slip away. "I had wished to speak to you." She turned to Mr. Carlyle. "I will join you, Mr. Ainsley, and Miss Grace in the music room as soon as possible."

The scowl Carlyle wore was satisfying, and with a small flourish, Roger extended his arm to his friend, and the two slipped out of the room to find their way to the garden.

"I have spoken to Miss Grace as you requested," Victoria began. "And you were correct that she is determined to marry – excessively determined. However, I believe I have convinced her that you are not perfect."

"She thought me perfect, did she?" Roger chuckled. He knew he was far from perfect, though he also knew he did cut a fine figure and had very charming manners — most times.

"He is perfect," Victoria said with a sigh while batting her lashes.

Roger laughed outright at that. The foolish actions of a young debutante became even more ridiculous when demonstrated by a lady as refined and sensible as his darling friend. "Which imperfection did you expose to her?"

They rounded a hedge and began down a path bordered by delicate flowers on one side and a great expanse of lawn on the other. There were a few couples making use of the lawn to sit and, Roger assumed, practice their musical numbers.

"Several," Victoria replied.

Roger pulled his eyes from observing the couples on the lawn to look at her. She was grinning broadly.

"However, Miss Grace did not seem to think your penchant for female companionship would be a problem for a wife."

"It would not be," Roger agreed. His time to be carefree was now and not when he had a wife and family.

"I was not aware of how seriously you viewed taking a wife." Her head dipped. "I am sorry. I should have considered how loyal you are to your family and friends, but I did not."

She had obviously heard his reasons for not wishing to marry. It was gratifying to hear her praise of him. Miss Tierney had praised him for his reasons when he had shared them at Heathcote that morning, and it had been quite pleasant to hear. However, it was far more gratifying hearing it from Victoria than it had been from Miss Tierney or would be from anyone else for that matter, for Victoria knew him best.

"The one item which Miss Grace could not reason away, however," Victoria continued, "was your view on educating your children at home. She is not keen to take on the task of education even if she is highly accomplished. Therefore, you will need to be adamant about a wife being an integral part of your children's education if you wish to keep her unfavourably disposed to pursuing you."

"Noted." That would not be a hardship, for he *was* adamant about his wife, just like himself, being involved with the development of their children's minds. "And have you discovered the gentleman with whom we might match her? Is it Ainsley?"

Victoria nodded. "He is one candidate. She also finds Mr. Ramsey appealing, and we discovered over a very long hour and a half of speaking to various gentleman that Mr. Yardley is not without his charms."

"Yardley, Ainsley, and Ramsey. Well done." He smiled at her. He had known she would not fail him. She never did. "And did you discover any gents who captured your fancy, my lady?"

She rolled her eyes just as he expected she would. However, her reply of "no" was not as quick in coming as he expected. It was almost as if she were pausing to consider some fellow before making her decision. Or perhaps, she was hiding the truth from him. That would make two secrets she held and would not share with him, and he did not like it one bit.

"I should go practice."

"Yes, we would not wish to make Carlyle wait," Roger grumbled.

He did not wish to return Victoria to the house. He wanted to make another, longer circuit of the garden with her at his side, but he would see her to the music room as she requested merely because she had requested it. Then, he would make his way to his room and while away his time lying on his bed, alone, with a book. It sounded dreadfully dull, but it was also the one place he knew he would not be called on to escort some lady on a walk or be expected to take part in empty conversations. How many times could he describe his estate? Or tell a lady which horse in his stable was his fastest or favourite?

"How long are you staying?" Victoria asked as they ascended the stairs to the music room.

"I had hoped three days at most, but if we are to see Miss Grace happily settled..."

"You do not think you can manage the feat in three days?" She teased.

He shook his head. Miss Grace did not appear to

be the quickest study and persuading a gentleman into marriage could prove to be tricky if the gentleman did not wish to be persuaded. Roger would have to discover which of the three candidates Victoria had mentioned was most eager to be settled into his future. As he considered these things, he and Victoria walked in companionable silence to the music room door.

"I am happy to have you here," she said.

He held the door partially open but closed it at her admission. "Why do you not yet wish to marry? I believe you have already heard my reasons."

She shook her head. "I just cannot tell you. I assure you that if I did, I would be embarrassed beyond recovery."

"Will you ever tell me?"

She drew in a breath and released it slowly as a maid scurried past them. "Maybe on the day I marry, for then it shall no longer matter."

He scowled. It was not the answer he had hoped to hear. He had thought she might tell him if they were at home. He had not thought she would make him wait so long as until her wedding day – which she had admitted was not something she was seeking to have happen any time soon.

"Perhaps I shall just have to find you a husband," he teased, though his heart was not truly in it. "Since that is the only way I shall ever know your secret." His heart was feeling rather bitter about that.

"Please, do not. I beg you."

He ignored the fear in her tone and continued on his teasing path. "Is there no one here who could charm you from your single state?"

Again, she unexpectedly paused before replying. "None who would have me."

Were those tears in her eyes? Bitterness fled and regret filled its place in his heart.

"I apologize. I have gone too far in my quest to know your secret, but we have shared so much." He wanted to wrap his arms around her and hold her close so that she could feel his remorse for causing her discomfort.

"One day," she whispered. "One day, perhaps we can share this secret as well."

He nodded and opened the door slowly. He would have to accept that for now.

"Are you well?" he asked as she passed him to enter the room.

"How can I be anything but well when you are here?" she said lightly.

He shook his head. "Seriously, Vic, are you well?"

"I would be better if I did not have to practice the piano, but yes, I am well. You have not upset me."

Perhaps he had not upset her, but his own heart was far from settled as he turned to seek the safety and solitude of his room.

Chapter 4

Victoria settled into a chair next to the piano and shuffled through the available sheets of music looking for a song that was familiar.

"Is my brother treating you well?" Diana Berkeley whispered as she took the chair next to.

Victoria glanced up from the pages she held and smiled at Roger's older sister, who had agreed to be her chaperone for this house party so that Victoria's mother would not have to attend. There was a young Berkeley boy who would be visiting Roger's mother, and since Mrs. Hamilton did not yet have any grandchildren, she had wished to help Mrs. Shelton enjoy her grandson.

"He always does," Victoria replied before turning her attention back to the sheets of music she held.

"What about that one?"

Victoria shook her head. "I am forever getting the timing wrong in the middle. If I were just playing, I could fudge my way through it, but that is not possible when someone is singing." She sighed.

"Is something amiss?"

"I do not wish to play."

"Then, why are you?" Diana was a lot like her brother in not bowing to the demands of others. If Diana had not wished to play. Diana would not have played.

Victoria shrugged.

"You felt guilty," Diana said.

It was not a question. It was a statement of fact. A very accurate statement of fact.

"I would not have told your mother."

"I have no doubt that Mrs. Abernathy would have seen to that duty for you. I could see it in the way she arched her brow at me when prodding me to play for Mr. Carlyle." Victoria lowered her voice and lifted a piece of music to hide behind as she whispered. "I confess that I was also fearful of how Mr. Carlyle would portray me to the other gentlemen."

"Are you considering any of them?"

"Not presently," Victoria replied. "However, one

must not paint herself as unyielding when she does not have the advantage of youth on her side."

She lowered the piece of music she had used as a shield. "I shall have to marry eventually, and I have not met every gentleman here. Most I have seen at one function or another in town, but I have not had an opportunity to converse with any of them. It would be foolish to hinder my chances over a piece of music."

"But I thought you were intent upon –"

"Yes, well," Victoria cut her off before she could finish her comment, "that is as likely to happen now as it has always been."

"You are not giving up hope, are you?"

"What do you think of Mr. Ainsley?" Victoria asked, ignoring her friend and chaperone's question.

"Does this mean you are giving up hope?" If Diana was anything, she was persistent. "Do you like Mr. Ainsley?"

"He is a very nice gentleman, but I am not asking for myself. Miss Grace, who has, as I understand it from Roger, spent some time at Stratsbury Park attempting to sway your brother from his single state, seems to think Mr. Ainsley might be a better alternative as a husband."

"Oh!" Diana's eyes grew wide as understanding dawned on her. "I have only heard good things about him from the other chaperones. His finances are good. His country estate is not lacking. He does have the care of his mother, but she is a dear lady – or so I have been led to believe. One can never be too certain with these chaperones. They might be trying to rid themselves of an unwanted prospect instead of speaking truthfully."

"This whole marrying business is a bit of a night-mare if you ask me. Does anyone truly know who she is marrying when she agrees to be wed?" Victoria shook her head in disgust. It was the part of the season she liked the least. It was difficult to discern the true intentions of anyone when a proper front must be displayed at all times. The length of a dance or a call in a drawing room was not enough time to learn much about someone. Topics were kept to the mundane and safe. One must not venture into areas of discussion that were of much substance.

"One does if she does not rush into it. Berkley and I knew each other for nearly a year before we were betrothed. Be patient. There is no need to have the thing decided by the end of this party. Unless, of course..." She smiled knowingly but did not finish her thought. She did not need to finish it, for she knew precisely where Victoria's heart lay.

"I have sung this one before." Mr. Carlyle, who was holding a sheet of music, had approached them. "'The True Lover's Farewell'," he said, presenting her with the music.

Victoria shook her head. "I am afraid I have never played that song." She picked up the music which lay on top of the pile on her lap. "This one I know quite well."

"'The Ash Grove'?" He eyed the piece. "It seems simple enough."

"It is not complex. Mr. Shelton and I have performed it several times. It is one of my father's favourites, and so he requests it often. I doubt I shall stumble at all while playing, for I shall be able to listen, and my fingers will just do as they have learned to do."

"It is a favourite of your father's, you say?"

The way Mr. Carlyle's eyebrows rose in curiosity caused Victoria to wonder if she should not have just accepted the new piece he had presented her.

His look was too calculating. It was as if he were considering how he might use this to impress her father or some such thing.

"And do you also like this song?" he asked.

Very much so, especially when Roger sang it. Mrs. Abernathy had not been wrong in her assessment of Mr. Shelton's ability to sing. However, that was not what she wished for Mr. Carlyle to know. She wanted Mr. Carlyle to know as little about her as possible, so she said, "It is a very pleasant song."

From the smile he wore, she knew he was satisfied with her answer.

"Then, it shall be perfect. Do you think we might try it now?" He motioned to the piano.

Victoria tamped down her irritation about having to play anything at all, handed the remaining sheets of music to Diana, and took her place at the instrument. The things one had to endure to please one's mother!

Thirty minutes later, once Mr. Carlyle, who was as exacting as she had imagined him to be, was satisfied with both his performance and hers, Victoria was allowed to quit her spot at the piano.

"Of all the frustrating, arrogant men!" she complained in a whisper to Diana. "Did you hear him instructing me on how best to play?"

Diana linked her arm with Victoria's. "I did. You bore it quite well." She glanced over her shoulder to where Mr. Carlyle still stood near the piano, singing the song to himself. "I rather think he might be considering you."

Victoria shuddered. "Please, do not accept any offers from him for anything. I shall take to my bed or be taken home early with a horridly contagious disease if necessary. I cannot abide such an imperious person!"

Diana chuckled. "Perhaps you should refuse to do as he says next time you meet so that he will know of your disgust of his fussiness. You gave him no reason to think you were anything but pleased to perform as directed. It was really not like you."

"He is the biggest gossip, Diana! I have heard him making mince of more than one lady."

"And if he were to say one bad thing about you, I would only need to tell my husband or my brother, and the man would be sorry for having ever even *thought* of you in a light that was not positive." She gave Victoria a stern look. "Do not let him lead if you do not wish to follow. That is it. Plain and simple."

Victoria sighed. Diana was correct, of course.

"If I had not heard him denigrating Miss Deighton last season..."

Diana gasped. "Is he the source of her troubles?"

Victoria nodded.

"Does my brother know this?"

"I could not say."

"I would think he does not if he allowed you to spend time with such a gentleman."

"Diana, I am nothing more than a friend to Roger. It would seem very strange if he did not allow me to spend time with other gentlemen." There was no reason for Roger to stand guard over her as if she were his.

"Little more than a friend," Diana scoffed.

Victoria gave her a pointed look, and she said no more.

Grace waved to them as they stood by the door and then turned to say something to Mr. Ainsley before hurrying over to join them. Neither Victoria nor Diana could leave without her. It would not do to leave a young woman alone in a room with two gentlemen and no chaperone.

"He is simply wonderful," Grace said when they had entered the hall. "His voice is divine. I am certain I could listen to him sing for hours, although he is perhaps not as good as Mr. Carlyle. You were very fortunate to have acquired such a good partner." She sighed. "And his care for how you played. I found it very touching." Her hand rested on her heart.

"I found it tiring," Victoria said. "He was condescending and overbearing."

"Then, you do not like him?" Grace looked at Victoria as if there were something wrong with her. "He is so handsome."

"I wish for more than a pretty face," Victoria replied. "I want someone who will treat me with respect, and I fear the only person Mr. Carlyle respects is Mr. Carlyle."

"How did Mr. Ainsley treat you?" Diana interjected.

"He was very kind. He asked after my comfort many times, and he excused all my mistakes while encouraging me to try again."

"You see!" Diana cried. "That is how a young man should treat a young lady. Mr. Ainsley is the sort of gentleman one should seek. Even if his eyes are not as deep a brown as Mr. Carlyle's and if, in terms of stature, he does not tower over any of the other men, his character sounds as if it is all that it should be."

"Do you really think so?" Grace asked eagerly.

"Yes," Diana answered firmly. "I have no doubt in my mind that Mr. Ainsley could make a fine husband for some young lady."

That seemed to make Grace think quite well of herself if one could judge such a thing from the lift of her chin and the smile on her lips.

"Do we still need to discover more about Mr. Yardley or Mr. Ramsey?" Victoria inquired.

"Hmmm." Grace's brow furrowed.

"I think it is a good idea if we do," Diana answered. "One does not select a hat without trying several, and I dare say it would be foolish to not consider the other gentlemen," she held up a finger, "unless, of course, your heart is engaged. Then, we must not waiver from our objective."

They stopped in front of the door to Victoria and Diana's room.

"Come," Diana said, "we will refresh ourselves and discover your heart's intent in our room." She opened the door. "I will send a message to your mother so that she does not worry about where you are. She was quite pleased to allow me to keep watch over you. I am certain she will not mind if I continue to do so."

Grace entered the room behind Diana. "Oh, I am sure she is far too busy with my sister. Felicity does like to sneak off at times." The young girl plopped down on the window seat. "This is an excellent view!"

"Yes, well," Diana said, "Victoria is not without a substantial fortune. An excellent view is expected."

Grace blinked as she turned to Victoria. "I had no idea you were an heiress."

"I would not say heiress," Victoria countered.

"I would," Diana said in a loud whisper. "But Victoria does not like to speak of such things. She finds them vulgar."

"I do not! I just think that a lady should be valued for more than the amount of money attached to her name."

"I am certain she should be, but that would not have gained us such a spacious room with such an excellent view."

"It really is a beautiful garden," Grace said.

"Mother, Felicity, and I have a room that overlooks the drive. It is the same room we use whenever we are visiting Miss Abernathy. She and Felicity are particular friends, you see."

"Pull the bell, please, Victoria," Diana said as she took a seat at the desk near the window. "This message must get sent to Mrs. Love straightaway. We would not wish for her to worry that her daughter has gone missing."

Victoria moved to do as requested while Grace set forth on an explanation of how her mother rarely worried about her. It was Felicity, it seemed, who was the cause for concern.

"And she was found in the garden – alone with Mr. Everett Clayton. She is fortunate that Mother was not there or the scolding that she would have had to endure would have been great indeed!" Grace leaned forward and whispered. "She was not wearing her bonnet, and her cheeks were very rosy when she returned to the house. She will not tell me what she was doing, but I am not so stupid as she thinks. I have heard what happens in dark corners of gardens."

To Victoria, it looked as if the young lady was

quite interested in what happened in those dark garden corners.

"Proper young ladies do not find themselves alone in gardens with gentlemen." Diana's tone was firm but gentle.

"Oh, no, of course not." A smile tipped the right side of Grace's mouth. "Unless she wishes to marry the gentleman."

Diana put down her pen. "Not even then," she said sternly. "It is a dangerous game your sister plays. A gentleman who is trapped is not a gentleman with whom it will be easy to live after the vows have been said."

"And then there are those gentlemen who will refuse to offer," Victoria added.

Grace gasped. "Are there really such gentlemen?"

"Sadly, yes," Diana said. "My brother would be one, I should think."

"Your brother?"

"Mr. Shelton," Victoria explained.

"Mr. Shelton is your brother?"

It was unlikely that the girl's eyes could grow any rounder than they were.

"He is, indeed. And I know for a fact that he

would not do what would be expected if he thought he had been trapped. He has a very peculiar notion of what is and is not honourable, and since a lady trapping a gentleman is not honourable, it justifies the gentleman in refusing to offer for her."

"But she would be ruined!" Grace cried.

"Most certainly," Diana agreed, "but such is the consequence for her duplicity. That is what he would say."

"I can hear him saying it," Victoria agreed.

Grace's mouth hung open for a full half minute before she snapped it closed. "And he wishes for a wife to help educate his children?"

Victoria nodded.

As Grace shook her head, a look of utter aghast bewilderment suffused her features, and Victoria knew, beyond a shadow of a doubt, that Roger was safe from the machinations of Miss Grace Love.

Chapter 5

"Good day, brother dear," Diana said as Roger took the chair next to her in the Abernathy's music room. "How have you been keeping yourself?" She lifted an eyebrow and gave him a teasing look.

He looked around the room before ducking his head closer to her ear and whispering, "I have been reading."

"Indeed?" There was a hint of laughter in her tone. "Mother will not be best pleased to hear you are secreting yourself away with a book when you should be looking for the future mother of her grandchildren."

"She has you for that," Roger returned. "Would you be increasing again?" He darted his eyes around the room once again as he whispered the question. "It would be a wonderful thing if you were since Mother would be too distracted with your health and all things infant to pay much attention to my single state."

"Really! Roger! You are going to have to come to the point someday, and you are not growing any younger, although the debutantes seem to be."

Roger sighed. "You mean they are growing younger, sillier, and harder to abide."

"That is precisely what I mean. I do not understand how some gentlemen can wait to marry until they are well into their thirties and seem content with a frivolous young thing." Her eye narrowed when Roger smirked. "You are incorrigible! There is more to marriage than the marriage bed."

"Why must you also assume I do not take the role of husband seriously?"

"Because you rarely appear serious about anything."

That was true. He could not fault her logic. He did like to sport a devil-may-care attitude. It was so much more enjoyable than being dour and somber.

Her shoulder bumped his when she leaned closer to ask, "Who else besides me has accused you of not taking the role of husband seriously?"

Roger scowled as he watched Victoria speaking to Carlyle.

"Victoria," he muttered.

How she could countenance a popinjay like Carlyle with such equanimity as to smile and look interested in whatever the man was saying was beyond him!

There were times to be polite and times to be disinterested. This was a time to affect an air of indifference. A lady did not present herself as attentive at a house party unless she wished to encourage the suit of a gentleman. There were far too many who were thinking very seriously about marrying at a gathering such as this for an appearance of attentiveness to any gentleman to be thought of as anything less than an incentive to pursue the obliging lady. Paying such marked attention, as Victoria seemed to be doing presently, was akin to drawing forth a ravenous lion by placing an injured and bleeding animal in front of it.

"I thought you enjoyed music," Diana said.

"I do."

"Then, you might wish to stop glaring as if you want to run through the next person to step up to the piano."

Perhaps he did not wish to gravely injure the *next*

person to perform, but there was Carlyle. Roger would not mind seeing that gentleman properly laid out on the lawn with some sort of wound.

"Mr. Carlyle has a lovely voice." Diana had followed Roger's glare and found the object of his discontent. "He is singing 'The Ash Grove' since Victoria is so familiar with that piece of music."

Roger's scowl deepened. That was the song he sang with Victoria.

"He was particularly interested to hear that the song is a favourite of Mr. Hamilton."

Roger eyed his sister skeptically.

"I did not tell him that. Victoria did." She sighed. "I think he is quite smitten with her, but then who could blame him. She is not flighty, she behaves just as a proper young lady should, and she is well-dowered. I know I am prejudiced, but Miss Hamilton is one of the best choices at this party."

"I would not argue with you about that," Roger muttered. "But *he* is not the best choice of gentleman." He turned his full attention back to his sister. "She could do far better than him."

Diana blinked. "How so?"

"He thinks far too well and too often of himself."

"An air of arrogance is not always a bad thing,"

Diana refuted. "He is confident. Confidence is a good quality to have in a husband."

"No," Roger grumbled. "He is not merely confident. He thinks of no one save himself. Would you have Victoria tied to a gentleman who does not consider her an equal or of enough importance to see to her needs ahead of his?"

Diana studied Mr. Carlyle for a moment before replying. "I suppose I would not, but if he is who makes Victoria happy, then who am I to stand in her way?"

"Her chaperone," the words rumbled from him.

Could his sister seriously not see what was wrong with a match between Carlyle and Victoria? He would expect such a thing from his mother, but he had always thought Diana to be more sensible than their mother when it came to making matches.

"As her chaperone, your job is to ensure she makes a good connection – one which will bring her the most advantage. And you know I do not speak of money or position. This is Vic. There are a good many things more important than riches and titles when seeing her settled."

His words had earned him the full attention of his sister.

"And what, pray tell," Diana asked, "is more important than a secure financial future?"

His eyes narrowed. "Her heart – as if you do not know." If he did not trust his sister as completely as he did, he would think she was leading him down a merry path.

"And Miss Grace? Do we wish to consider her heart as well when we are scheming?"

"As long as her heart is not set on me, you may do anything you wish with it."

She was nowhere near Roger or even looking in his direction, yet he could feel the disapproval of Victoria at such a statement. He sighed.

"It would, I suppose, be best if we took care not to damage the young lady's heart."

There. Surely, that would satisfy both his sister and Victoria.

"Mr. Ainsley seems a good candidate. He was quite attentive to Miss Grace while they were practising, and he seems a respectable sort of fellow. I shall do my best to encourage them to spend some time together if I can," his sister whispered.

That was good. He turned to say something of that nature to his sister.

"And then, I shall have to decide upon someone to recommend to Victoria since you do not think Mr. Carlyle will do."

"Victoria is in no hurry to marry," he protested.

His sister raised a skeptical brow.

"She said so."

"What a lady says and what she truly thinks are not always the same."

Roger crossed his arms. "Vic is not one of those ladies."

"If you say so," his sister whispered as the first young lady took her place at the piano.

He did say so. He knew so. Victoria always told him what she thought – often more directly than was entirely proper. Of course, that was typically because he had provoked her to it. He shook his head. No. If Victoria were intent upon finding a husband, she would have said something.

His eyes narrowed as Carlyle leaned toward Victoria and whispered something.

"If it must be done, then choose anyone but Carlyle," he whispered to his sister.

"Will you help me?"

He shrugged. Could he help her? He had no desire to see Victoria marry just yet. He enjoyed her friendship too much to wish her taken from him. Oh, he would still be allowed to visit her, but it would not be the same as meeting on a nearly daily basis.

"I will consider it." That was the best he could offer his sister at present. No, that was not the best he could do. "Present your ideas of who might be a good option to me before you say anything to Victoria. I will vet them. No fortune hunters. No gentlemen who care more about their horses or jacket than anything else. And no scoundrels."

Victoria deserved only the best husband.

Roger joined in the polite applause around him and settled back to listen to the next selection while discounting each and every gentleman in attendance as not good enough for his darling friend.

~*~*~

"There are lemonade and sweets set up in the garden," Mrs. Abernathy said when the last musician had risen from the piano.

"Oh, how fortuitous," Diana exclaimed. "I had expected the gentlemen to scuttle off to some activity while we females would be left to stitch in the drawing room. And that is not conducive to making matches. I really do not know why more hostesses do not plan an abundance of activities to keep the ladies and gentlemen together at these things." She rose and took her brother's arm. "How are sparks to be ignited if the individuals whom we wish to have matched are kept apart? It seems very backward to the purpose of a house party. Would you not agree?"

"I would not dare to disagree," Roger replied with a smile. "However, I must say I enjoy the times of separation, for often the chaperones are not as attentive in those moments, and... well... ladies can be persuaded to steal away for a few moments."

She swatted his arm. "Really, Roger! You are a rogue."

"Only because I am not yet ready to marry," Roger refuted.

"Over there," Diana pointed to the left with her fan. "Mr. Carlyle is absconding with my charge." Her lips twitched.

Roger wished to argue with her that it was not truly absconding if they were all headed to the same place, but he did not because it was far more important to him that they reach Carlyle and Victoria quickly. The less time Victoria spent alone with that gentleman, the better.

"Mr. Shelton, Mrs. Berkeley," Miss Grace called to them.

Roger groaned at the delay the young lady posed.

"Was it not the best afternoon of music ever?" she cried when they approached.

"Oh, it was amongst the best I have attended," Diana agreed. "You sang beautifully, Mr. Ainsley."

"Thank you." He smiled at Grace. "My accompanist was quite good."

"Delightfully so," Diana said.

"To be sure," Roger muttered as he attempted to see through the door to the garden and catch a glimpse of Victoria.

"Miss Hamilton played beautifully, as well," Mr. Ainsley continued. "Simple songs are often the most enjoyable."

Roger eyed the gentleman. Was he complimenting Victoria while he had Grace on his arm for any particular reason? It would be a very shabby thing indeed if Ainsley were flattering another lady with hopes of securing some support from her chaperone while in the presence of a lady such as Grace who so obviously admired him.

Roger took a moment to imagine skewering the gentleman with a pointed question regarding his intentions. The thought of Ainsley squirming at such a question cause Roger's lips to tip up with amusement even as he once again attempted to see Victoria through the open garden door while his sister went on and on about favouring simple musical selections over grand arias.

"I think there is a time and a place where each is best," Miss Grace said. "Do you not agree, Mr. Shelton?"

Roger returned his attention to his group. "I could not say as I was considering the refreshment to be found in a glass of lemonade rather than attending to your conversation."

"Oh!" Grace cried. "Do not let us detain you any longer."

"Thank you." He really could not get out to the garden quickly enough.

"Join us," Diana invited. "I really should find my charge and congratulate her on a job well done."

It took very little time to find Victoria when they finally reached the garden. Pleasantries – tiring pleasantries – were exchanged along with congratulations from one lady to another and back.

"Mr. Carlyle, your performance was divine," Mrs. Abernathy cooed as she came to inspect the table upon which the refreshments were laid. "We really should have you sing with my Amelia when next there is an opportunity. Her abilities would highlight yours so well."

"I am not certain I can give up Miss Hamilton. She was very accommodating, and I would not wish to snub her."

A fine, gallant, yet not entirely so, response, Roger thought as he hid his scowl behind the rim of his glass.

"Do not let me hold you back," Victoria said.

Roger's scowl turned into a smile at her words.

"I am certain I have played the only song I would feel comfortable playing," Victoria continued. "Therefore, if Miss Abernathy is willing and there is another time to display your musical talent, please do not let me stop you from doing so."

The cad took her hand! Roger wished to yank it away from him!

"Are you certain? I should not wish you to think my admiration fleeting."

Why would she smile so pleasantly at such a statement? Did she not know that doing so was far too encouraging to the likes of Carlyle? Unless... it was not possible. Victoria simply could not mean to encourage Carlyle.

"I am positive, Mr. Carlyle."

Roger sighed softly in relief. At least she had not said something like *I could never think your admiration fleeting*. Her answer — a polite response without being indulgent — proved his point. She was not interested in snaring Carlyle.

Mrs. Abernathy clapped her hands. "Excellent. One evening after dinner we will have to have some music. It will be imperative." She turned her eyes on Roger. "Perhaps you will favour us with a song, Mr. Shelton?"

"No," Roger replied between sips of lemonade. "I have no intention of singing."

"Oh, I am not easily dissuaded, Mr. Shelton. I shall work on you until you agree."

"It will never happen," Roger replied with a smile. "I am quite a stubborn old goat."

Victoria's lips pressed together, but her eyes were laughing.

Mrs. Abernathy shook her head. "That is what

all gentlemen think at one point or another, but few truly are as stubborn as they declare. I shall not be discouraged, Mr. Shelton."

Thankfully, she turned away from him to Mr. Carlyle.

"Now, Mr. Carlyle. If you would be so good as to lend me your arm, we shall tell my Amelia the good news. She was quite taken with your singing; I assure you."

Carlyle gave Victoria an apologetic look but extended his arm to Mrs. Abernathy and allowed her to lead him away.

Roger took another sip of his lemonade. Perhaps if Mrs. Abernathy could dispose of Mr. Carlyle and his *admiration*, then Roger might be persuaded by gratitude to favour her with a song.

Chapter 6

"Mr. Clayton!" Grace greeted the gentleman with great animation as she and Victoria approached him.

Mr. Ainsley had excused himself from Grace's side some minutes ago, and Roger was being a dutiful brother and escorting his sister as she followed behind her charge and Miss Grace Love.

"Miss Grace," Mr. Everett Clayton replied with a small bow.

"You must meet my friend, Miss Hamilton," Grace said. "And her chaperone, Mrs. Berkeley. She is Mr. Shelton's sister. And, of course, you know Mr. Shelton. Is it not exciting that we are able to be together here just as we were when I was at Heathcote?"

"Indeed, it is." The gentleman's reply was accompanied by a polite smile but not one which spoke to Victoria of him genuinely being delighted to be where he was at the moment.

Grace looked around as if something were missing. "Where is my sister?"

Mr. Clayton's smile wavered. "With your mother and Mrs. Abernathy, I believe."

"Well, then, you must join us," Grace offered. "We are not a big party, but a stroll through the garden and the wilderness beyond is much more pleasant when accompanied by friends. Is it not, Mr. Shelton?"

"Not particularly," Roger grumbled, earning a swat of his arm from his sister. He scowled at her. "Did you wish for me to lie?"

"Yes," Diana replied. "There is a time and a place for abject honesty. This is not one of them."

"You and mother," he grumbled under his breath.

"I think it can be a wonderful thing to be surrounded by friends," Diana said to Grace. "And I am certain Roger is happy to see you again, Mr. Clayton." She raised an eyebrow at her brother.

"Of course, I am not disappointed to see you, Clayton," Roger admitted. "That was not my meaning."

"Then was your meaning that you preferred not to be in company with us ladies?" Victoria knew she likely shouldn't ask such a thing, but the opportunity to unsettle Roger when he had been what she would consider to be rude was just too tempting to ignore.

Roger pressed his lips together and looked at his sister. "Of course not," he lied.

Victoria knew he was lying for he said the words with that particular smile he wore when he was avoiding being scolded. She caught her breath as the smile slipped into something more calculating and grimaced even before he opened his mouth, for she knew that whatever was going to be said was designed to be shocking.

"I find wandering in the wilderness with ladies – or, more precisely, *a* lady – to be a particularly enjoyable pastime. So much can be learned about life and nature during such a stroll." He batted his eyes three times at Victoria, daring her to scold him for his innuendo.

"Do you collect flowers and leaves and press them in books?" Grace asked.

There was nothing but innocent curiosity in her expression. Oh, the girl was in desperate need of education before she was ready to seriously consider marriage. Victoria sent a pleading look to Diana, while Mr. Clayton attempted to recover from a sudden coughing spell.

"My brother is not speaking of proper pursuits," Diana said softly.

"Then, of what is he –" Grace's question stopped abruptly. Her eyes grew wide as her cheeks flushed a brilliant red. Apparently, she had deciphered Roger's meaning.

"He is very wicked to speak of such a thing in the presence of ladies," Victoria assured her young friend. "He is an absolute scoundrel."

Roger had the decency to look somewhat censured.

"He just has not yet found the right lady with whom to walk and behave appropriately," Diana added. "It is how it is with some gentlemen. They are nothing but rogues and rascals until they find a reason to be otherwise. Quite often it is a lady who compels such a change."

"Yes, yes," Grace said quite seriously. "Mr. Shelton has said as much himself."

"When did I admit to such foolishness?" Roger demanded.

"Why at Heathcote! Do you not remember our discussion about why you did not wish to marry?"

"Indeed?" Diana said with much interest.

Roger's expression twisted as if he had been poked by a hot iron.

"Oh, yes!" Grace continued. "Mr. Shelton fully intends to give up his current ways, which I now understand to be excessively improper, when he marries. However, he is not ready to do that just yet. And my cousin, Miss Tierney, said that he would no longer fear giving up his freedom when he met a lady who claimed his heart and caused him to fear losing her more than he feared losing his reprobate lifestyle." She batted her lashes and gave Roger a pointed look.

Victoria bit back a smile. It appeared that though Miss Grace tended to ramble on at a fairly rapid pace, she was not without the ability to hide a reprimand within a pleasantly delivered bit of information.

"So, Clayton, how are you finding this gathering?" Roger, who looked eager to leave their current topic of conversation, motioned to the path ahead of them, indicating they should walk on. "Is it all you had hoped?"

The gentleman's polite smile was back. "It is difficult to say since we have only been here a short time. However, the music this afternoon was delightful."

This set Grace on a course of admiration for all the musical selections – *again*. Victoria smiled and nodded just as she had the first two times when Grace had shared her raptures about the musicale.

Indeed, it was Grace who bore the greatest share of the conversation as they continued down the path, past the grand old tree with a bench beneath it, around the loop where the path turned at the stream, and back to where the others were gathered on the lawn.

Victoria was excessively relieved when Diana suggested that Grace should make certain her mother was not missing her.

"My ears are weary," Roger muttered as he dropped onto the lawn next to Victoria when Diana and Grace were well away from them.

"Miss Grace does possess a great talent for conversation," Victoria agreed.

"Her sister is little better," Mr. Clayton, who had joined them, added.

Victoria looked at her companions uneasily.

"I thought you and she were destined to be married," Roger said easily as he leaned back and propped himself up on his elbows.

"Are you certain you wish to discuss this here?" Victoria inserted. This seemed like a conversation that should be held between gentlemen when they were far removed from ladies.

"It is not a secret," Roger replied. "I am certain Miss Grace has mentioned Miss Love and Mr. Clayton's attachment." He looked toward where his sister was walking with Grace. "She must have said something. I cannot imagine her keeping silent about such a thing."

"Well, yes, she has mentioned it," Victoria admitted, "but it was done in the privacy of my room and not in the garden."

"How many were in your room?" Roger queried. "Three people?"

Victoria nodded.

"Then, the only thing different between Miss Grace telling you about her sister and Mr. Clayton's attachment and my mentioning it now is our location," he concluded before turning back to Mr. Clayton.

"I thought we were destined to be married as

well," Mr. Clayton replied. "However, I had little competition at Stratsbury Park. My brother would not give Miss Love a second look, and Max was her cousin. So, I was the logical choice, you see." He blew out a breath. "However, at a house party with so many gentlemen of fortune, as this party has, a clergyman's living seems to lack the polish necessary to hold her attention."

"Has she broken off with you?" Victoria whispered.

Mr. Clayton shook his head. "Not yet, but I expect it."

"That is dreadful!"

"Is it?" Mr. Clayton asked. "Or is it fortuitous? I hardly know, although, presently, I will admit that I find it rather dreadful."

"Of course, you do," Roger assured him. "But that does not mean it will always be as it is now. She might just be having a bit of fun and will realize that no one else measures up to you."

Mr. Clayton shook his head. "Graeme warned me about her. Apparently, she was quite the flirt during the season. I thought my brother was just being my brother." He shrugged.

"I helped Graeme secure his current lady, you know," Roger said.

Mr. Clayton laughed. "Did you? I cannot say that I noticed."

"That is because you noticed nothing aside from Miss Love when I was at Stratsbury Hall," Roger retorted. "However, a little flirting with Miss Tierney and the threat of pursuing her myself were what brought him to the point."

"That is how you arranged a match?" Victoria shook her head. "I fear that does not make you a matchmaker at all."

"It most certainly does!"

"And are you going to flirt with Miss Grace to make Mr. Ainsley take notice?"

"You are attempting to match Miss Grace with Ainsley?" Mr. Clayton asked in surprise.

Both Victoria and Roger nodded.

"Good luck to you both," Mr. Clayton continued, "I hear he has a beauty back home who will not be out until next season, but he has promised to wait for her."

"No!" Victoria cried. "Are you certain?"

Mr. Clayton nodded.

"Then, what are we to do? Miss Grace finds him

very attractive as a possible suitor." Of all the rotten luck! Victoria looked to Roger for an answer, but he only shrugged and shook his head.

"There were some others she mentioned," Victoria said after a few moments of silence. "How did you not know this?" she demanded of Roger. "You were supposed to find out things about the gentlemen she listed."

"And when have I had the opportunity?" Roger argued. "I spent the time you were practising with Carlyle in my room and then I have been with you, my sister, and Miss Grace ever since."

He had a point. "Very well, I will allow you that," she said.

"You would not trade the elder sister for the younger one, would you, Clayton? Miss Grace is a bit of a chatterbox, but she seems trustworthy, if a trifle naïve."

"A trifle?" Victoria muttered, causing Roger's left eyebrow to cock in question, though he said nothing.

"I am afraid I cannot oblige you in such a fashion," Mr. Clayton answered.

"Are you certain?"

"Really, Roger!" Victoria exclaimed. "The gentleman's heart is not free at present to consider anyone."

"My apologies, Clayton."

"I am not offended."

Roger flopped back onto the grass and placed his hat over his eyes. "You will keep me safe from marauding females if I fall asleep, will you not?"

"Perhaps," Victoria replied.

Roger lifted his hat and looked at her. She smiled in return, and he once again put his hat over his eyes. She would not let anyone accost him – at least, not anyone he did not wish to have accost him. The thought of him finally choosing someone to be his wife pricked her heart.

"You would not consider a parson, would you, Miss Hamilton?"

"No, she would not," Roger said from beneath his hat.

"I think I can speak for myself," Victoria retorted. "I am not opposed to the profession, but I am not certain I am best suited for the position of parson's wife. However, if I were to find myself enamoured with a gentleman who was destined to be the caretaker of a parish, I am certain I would be able to find my footing. After all, I am not unfamiliar with serving the tenants on my father's estate. I would imagine being a parson's wife would be somewhat similar in some regards?"

"Most likely," Mr. Clayton replied with a nod.

He looked so forlorn. She had yet to meet Miss Grace's sister, but Victoria was certain she would not like the young woman. How could any lady toy with the heart of a gentleman who seemed as pleasant and obliging as Mr. Clayton?

"I am certain that, in time, you will find the right lady to fill the role of Mrs. Clayton," she assured him. "And," she added with a whisper, "I would not discount Miss Grace just because her sister has treated you ill. Grace is talkative, but she is the sort of young lady whom I do not mind claiming as a friend."

"You are very kind, Miss Hamilton."

"That she is," Roger muttered from under his hat.

"And I would be happy to count you among my friends as well, Mr. Clayton, so if you are in need of a partner for a game of cards or for a dance or some such thing, I do hope you will consider asking me."

Roger's hat lifted from his eyes, but Victoria

ignored him, choosing instead to smile at Mr. Clayton, who was thanking her for her offer.

If jealousy could work on Roger's friend, then maybe, it could also work on him. She would not toy with Mr. Clayton. She was not the sort of lady to do such a thing. However, marriage could not be put off forever, and before she began searching in earnest elsewhere, she needed to know if she had any hope in securing the heart of the gentleman who had held hers for most of her life.

Chapter 7

"We will start from the top of the table, of course, with Amelia." Mrs. Abernathy waited for her daughter to join her where she stood near the door to the drawing room in which all the houseguests were gathered to wait for dinner.

"Shall we see who it is who will dine with you?"

Miss Abernathy said an eager yes as her mother shook a bowl containing several small pieces of paper. She swirled her hand inside the bowl and pulled out a name. "Oh! How delightful! Mr. Carlyle."

The gentleman straightened his jacket, crossed the room, and offered his arm to Miss Abernathy, whose waited only until her daughter and Mr. Carlyle had left the room before looking around and calling Victoria forward.

Of all the inane ideas! Roger crossed his arms

and leaned against the wall near the window. The woman was obviously assigning gentleman dinner partners at random, but she was proceeding through the ladies based on status. Victoria was well-dowered. It was not something she published nor was it a fact she kept secret. He glowered at two gentlemen who had started whispering when Victoria's name was called. He did not like it. His friend did not need any fortune hunters scampering after her.

"Mr. Clayton," Mrs. Abernathy said.

Roger blew out a breath. It could be worse. She could have been stuck with Carlyle or one of those whispering gents.

Lady after lady was summoned forward and gentleman after gentleman was assigned as a partner.

"Is this not the best?" Grace said as she took Roger's arm. "It is such a surprise! I do like surprises."

"I do not," Roger replied.

Grace giggled. "I will admit I had hoped I would be assigned someone different."

"I hear Ainsley has a chit waiting for him at home," Roger whispered.

Grace's smile slid into a frown. "Does he indeed?"

"I have not asked him, of course, but that is what I have heard. We should proceed with caution."

She tipped her head. "What do you mean *we?*"

That had not been well-thought-out. He had forgotten that Miss Grace was not in on the scheme to see her married. "You seemed fond of him, and I had thought to help you in securing him."

"That is very kind of you, Mr. Shelton."

"Think nothing of it. Anything for a friend of Miss Hamilton."

"She is very nice," Grace said as they waited for the remaining couples to enter the dining room.

"The best," Roger replied, looking down the table to where she sat across from Miss Abernathy and next to Everett Clayton. She was smiling and leaning her head toward Clayton to hear what the fellow was saying. Truly, she needed to learn some restraint. Such open interest even for a chap thought by many to be firmly secured by Miss Love was not wise. Tongues would wag, and chaperones would scheme.

Grace touched his arm. "Are you fond of her?"

He nodded. "We have been friends for longer than I can remember. My first memory of our friendship was when I brought her a toad and placed it in a teacup on this little table that she had which she would lay out all properly with a cloth and imaginary biscuits."

"A toad!" Grace giggled. "And what did she do?"

Roger chuckled. "She nodded her head in greeting and instructed Mr. Brown – that is what she named him – that he was not to spill his tea or eat all the biscuits. And then, she proceeded to instruct me with the same rules and scolded me for my dirty hands. She has been scolding me ever since."

Grace giggled but pressed her lips together as Mrs. Abernathy entered with her husband and took her place.

"My hands are clean, I assure you," Roger whispered to Grace as a bowl of soup was placed before him.

"I shall have to thank Miss Hamilton for having taught you such good manners," Grace teased.

He glanced down the table at Victoria once again. She had taught him many things over the years. Was there ever a better friend that anyone could have? She leaned toward Clayton again. Roger caught his scowl before it could form and turned back to his soup.

"If she is such a good friend," Grace whispered, "why do we not attempt to find her a husband? Every young lady needs one eventually."

"She does not wish to marry just yet," Roger answered.

"But she does look very pretty sitting next to Mr. Clayton and talking as she is. I know he has his heart set on my sister, but..." she let her words fall away, replacing them with a simple shrug.

Victoria looked pretty no matter who was sitting next to her or whether she was talking, being silent, or scolding him. Roger applied himself to eating his soup and attempted to keep his eyes from wandering too often down to where his friend sat.

"There are other gentlemen."

Grace did not seem ready to give up the idea of seeing Victoria matched with some gentleman at this party.

"Not Mr. Carlyle, of course," she added quickly. "He was very demanding when they were practising, and Miss Hamilton said that such behaviour indicates a gentleman who will not be an attentive husband." She slurped a spoonful of soup. "And every lady wishes for an attentive husband, do you not think?"

Roger nodded his head as he scooped the last spoonful of soup from his bowl. It was a small comfort to know that Carlyle was not someone Victoria admired, no matter how much the gentleman had seemed interested in her earlier.

"Tell me, Miss Grace, what do you wish for in a husband? If I am to help you find one, I must know a thing or two about what you would prefer."

"But," she protested in a whisper as her soup bowl was taken away, "we have not settled on a match for Miss Hamilton."

Roger had no desire to settle on a match for Victoria. The very idea of her marrying anyone made him wish to refuse the venison placed before him, and, if anyone knew him as well as Victoria knew him, they would know that venison was among his most favoured foods.

"I believe since she is not so desirous to marry as you are, it might be best if we decide upon a match for you before we attempt to arrange something for Miss Hamilton."

"Do you truly think that would be best?"

"Yes." He was very sure of it.

"Very well," Grace said, and, while Roger savoured his venison and occasionally glanced in Victoria's direction, Grace enumerated all the qualities she wished for in a husband.

~*~*~

"She actually cares about how she will be treated and not just how he looks or what style of architecture his house is," Roger said later to his sister. He blew out a breath. "She is not completely without sense." The fact still surprised him. He had not, to this point, thought that Grace possessed any great amount of substance, and he still did not think she possessed much. However, she was not without some depth.

"She also informed me that Mr. Carlyle is not a good choice for Victoria, which I believe I already told you, but I think it is good that you have the information from more than one source."

"Mr. Clayton would be better," Diana agreed.

That was not what Roger had meant. His brow furrowed. The two – Clayton and Victoria – had spent a great deal of time together this evening.

First, there had been supper, and then, there had been cards.

"He is not available," Roger said as he watched Victoria take a turn of the drawing room on the man's arm.

"Not yet, but I have heard rumors that he might be... and soon."

"Where did you hear this?" If it was from Victoria, it was news that was no better than Roger already knew.

"A couple of the other chaperones were discussing it in hushed tones earlier. It seems Mr. Walcott or Mr. Ramsey might be more to Miss Love's liking." She leaned close enough to her brother that her shoulder pressed into his. "Their incomes are substantial."

That information seemed to match nicely – unfortunately so – with what Clayton had said. How did Miss Grace have a sister who was so calculating and cunning? The two ladies seemed to be exact opposites, yet he had heard Grace praise her sister as if Felicity were a goddess capable of no wrong. He shook his head. The chit was more than a trifle naïve just as Victoria had insinuated earlier today.

"Mr. Ainsley's heart is not unfettered," Roger said, his mind still focused on the better of the Love sisters. "I have mentioned it to Miss Grace."

His sister's eyes grew wide.

"Clayton says the gentleman has a lady waiting for him at home. She is not yet out, but there seems to be some sort of arrangement."

"Since he is here, his mother must either not be in favor of the match, or she is unaware." Diana sighed. "Neither speaks well of him, in my opinion."

"His mother might be unreasonable. Remember how our mother was when you were first out. There was not a gentleman in all of London who was deemed good enough for her daughter. Even Berkley struggled to win Mother's approval."

"But he has it now."

"Because he has provided her with a grandchild," Roger muttered.

Diana jabbed him with her elbow. "She liked him before Thomas was born."

"But you must admit she likes him even better now."

Diana chuckled. "She does, and her admiration of him will only grow as our family does." She shook her head at Roger's teasing smile. "No, I am not increasing." She flicked open her fan. "Not that I am avoiding it," she added.

Roger laughed out loud at that. His sister may pretend to be shocked by his improper behaviour, but she was not so far removed from it herself. On two occasions in their lifetime, he had come across her in the garden late at night sneaking into the house just as he was sneaking out. Of course, she had been out to go swimming while his purpose was not so innocent. However, the truth of the matter remained, she was not so flawless as she might like to appear.

"Now, if I wish to keep Mother happy..." She scanned the room. "Who here would meet her expectations for you?"

Roger shook his head. "Leave off, Diana. I am not here to find a wife."

"Humor me," she cajoled. "Discussing possibilities with you is a great deal more fun than discussing them with the other chaperones." Again, she flicked open her fan. "Not one of them has yet mentioned any physical attributes – only fortunes and estates. A secure future is a good thing, do not get me wrong, but truly, one must think about whose bed she will be warming to do her duty."

Roger shook his head and chuckled. "And is that why you chose Berkley?"

Her cheeks flushed. "I was not unaware of how warm his bed could be when we married," she whispered.

Roger turned startled eyes to her. "Indeed? I am not the only rake?"

"I do prefer the term rake to what Mother would call me, but no, I did not warm bed after bed, my dear brother."

"Only Berkley's?"

She shrugged. "Only once... or twice. But that is not what we were discussing, and you will not mention that to Mother. Ever. Or I will have Berkley hurt you."

Roger chuckled. "I would not dream of telling Mother unless greatly provoked."

"Now, how many of these ladies capture your fancy?"

Roger looked around the room. There were lithe figures as well as pleasantly curved ones. There were ladies with golden hair and those with tresses of toffee and chocolate. There was even one beauty who wore her flaming locks very well. Some were tall and would be able to nearly look him in the eye without rising onto their toes to do so, and then there were those who would be perfectly sized to snuggle into his side and listen to his heart. Nearly all of them had fair complexions, even if their beauty varied by degrees. There were several whom he should be attempting to charm, for they had very kissable pouts. However, not one of them made him pause long enough to seriously consider her. He shook his head.

"The same number who would meet with Mother's approval," he said in answer to his sister's question.

"One," Diana said.

"No, none," Roger corrected.

Diana gave the smallest shake of her head before tipping it toward the door to the garden. "One," she repeated.

Roger's eyes followed her head tip. There standing at the door was Victoria.

"You said you would allow me to present any possible matches for her to you for approval, and I am."

Him? Marry Victoria?

"Think about it," Diana whispered before rising and leaving him to do just that.

Chapter 8

Victoria's morning ride had been as delightful as any ride through the countryside could be. The sun was shining in a nearly solid blue sky as only a few clouds were dotting the expanse above. The air was fresh and not at all close. The only thing which had dampened the enjoyment of the exercise had been that it was entirely too short. Well, maybe that was not the only thing which had not met with Victoria's satisfaction. There had been one thing — or rather, one person — missing.

"Have you seen Roger today?" Victoria had slipped into the library and had taken a seat next to Diana on a sofa.

"He said good morning to me," Diana replied, looking up from her book. "He was dressed to go riding. I assumed he was going with the group."

"He was not with us." Victoria pulled her lower

lip between her teeth. He could be anywhere. He had spoken of escaping after a few days of being at the house party when he first arrived, but then, when they had decided to help Grace find a match, he had said he would be required to stay longer. "Did he leave?" she whispered behind her book.

There was worry in the wide eyes that met Victoria's question. "I will ask."

Victoria put a hand on Diana's arm to keep her from rising. "No, please do not. He may have wished to slip away unnoticed, and I should hate for him to become the topic of gossip due to my curiosity."

"It is not as if his absence will not be noted and remarked on," Diana argued. "It is best to know now if we shall have to endure such whispers."

Diana covered Victoria's hand with her own. "I will only be a moment, and I shall be as discreet as possible." One of her eyebrows arched. "I should like to know if my little brother is fulfilling his duty to his mother or not."

Victoria could not help smiling at Diana's stern tone. Diana would likely lecture Roger about his disappearance, but she would not tell their mother. The two had always kept each other's secrets. It was a far different sort of relationship that they had than Victoria had with her older brother. He had often found it necessary to tell their mother or father if he found Victoria doing something she was not supposed to be doing. Not that those moments were frequent. Victoria did not like to stray outside of the rules too often. She did not always agree with the guidelines in which she was to live, but she did not wish to be found wanting in any way. Therefore, she suppressed her displeasure and behaved as was expected.

Of course, both her mother and father were not severe in their adherence to societal expectations, and that did make for a great deal less displeasure on Victoria's part. Unlike some in the upper circles, her parents were welcoming of new arrivals – even those who had made their fortune rather than inheriting it. And while Victoria had had all the proper education a young lady should receive from a governess, her parents had also encouraged Victoria to learn all she wished to learn on any subject she chose.

Neither her father nor her mother had ever kept her from exploring books on flora and fauna nor had they kept her from reading her fill of novels.

Had she been the sort of lady given to excessive imagination and dramatics she might have found her reading materials restricted, for her mother could not and would not abide anyone who was melodramatic.

Sense should always rule over sensibility, according to Mrs. Hamilton, and in that way, Victoria was much like her mother. It was why she could sit here now, wondering where Roger was, without feeling to great a need to go to the window and watch for him — even if one could see the entry from the second window on the wall facing the front of the house and it had a very inviting chair near it. She would remain where she was and apply herself to her purpose for being in the library.

Victoria opened her book and picked up the lavender ribbon used to hold her place. This had been the ribbon Roger had given her when she was twelve and had just discovered that one could like a neighbour boy much more than one might like a brother. She smiled as she remembered the discussion she had had with Diana about that very thing.

Obviously, there was no way Victoria was going to ask for an explanation from her mother about why her heart seemed to race and her cheeks flushed when Roger smiled at her. Nor was she going to reveal to her mother that, occasionally, Roger kissed Victoria in her dreams. However, Diana, who was a very wise seventeen at the time, had seemed the best person to ask. She was, of course, facing her first season, and so she knew so much more about gentlemen and hearts and the dreary feelings that permeated a young lady's very soul when a favoured gentleman left to attend school.

Diana had insisted upon Victoria telling her who the young man was who had captured Victoria's affections, and Victoria had feared that Diana would not approve of her liking Roger. However, on that account, Victoria had been most assuredly wrong for Diana had actually been quite delighted with the idea that one day they might be sisters.

Of course, even now, Diana still hoped one day they might be, but if Victoria were completely honest with herself about Roger – something she had been attempting to be more and more lately – she would have to admit that the possibility seemed less likely than it ever had. Roger still treated her as a special friend, but he never attempted to flirt with her or kiss her. He never had. In fact, he had never even seemed to feel it awkward to embrace her on occasion. It appeared as if Victoria was little different than Diana in Roger's eyes.

"He has not left," Diana whispered as she smoothed her skirts after returning to her spot on the couch. "He is just gone off by himself. He does that you know."

Victoria nodded.

"And from a quick look in the drawing room and a glance into the garden, it appears there are no young ladies missing from our party." She shrugged when Victoria looked at her in surprise. "It is Roger."

Could three words spoken with a tone of regret cut a heart more deeply? It was a good thing Victoria was not given to dramatics, or she might take herself off to her room to have a good cry over the idea of Roger seeming to prefer every lady to her. Or so it appeared from the way he spoke of the debutants in town and the ones he had met while at school.

"To be fair," Diana continued almost as if she could read Victoria's mind, "it has been some time since I have heard any scandalous whispers regarding my brother. I had hoped it was a sign that he was finally coming to the point, but..." she let her thought trail off.

Victoria had hoped the same when she saw him arrive at the Abernathy's, for he had immediately asked about her location. She had heard him. However, he had only arrived to deliver presents to her from himself and her father. He was merely seeing to the well-being of a friend. He was good at that. She had heard him speak of a few close friends and how he was going to help this one or that one with some project. She sighed. He had even helped one become engaged. Yet, he seemed none too willing to consider marriage himself.

"Are there any gentlemen here whom you might recommend?" she asked Diana.

"Besides my brother?"

Victoria nodded as she swallowed the sorrow that rose at the thought. "I must start considering other possibilities."

"Are you certain? You are only three and twenty."

"Only?" Victoria said in a scoffing tone. "I am a veritable old maid compared to the rest of the hopeful ladies here. I dare say the next oldest is a very ancient nineteen."

"No, no. Miss Hannington is twenty."

"That is still three years younger than me," Victoria argued. "So, you see my point."

"Not completely," Diana insisted.

"I doubt I will be invited to many more of these parties."

"That is not a bad thing," Diana whispered. "I have never understood the appeal of a house party. There are eight gentlemen here – eight! Out of the hundreds that live in England, you and the others are expected to consider making a match with these eight gentlemen because their parents are friends with Mr. and Mrs. Abernathy, or they are relations like Mr. Danvers.

"I must admit that Mrs. Abernathy has not chosen paupers. I think Mr. Clayton might have the smallest income, and his is not unreasonably low. However, that is not my point. My point is that there are only eight gentlemen here. And," she leaned closer and gave a look around the room before continuing, "there is no guarantee that any of them will capture your heart. A healthy income is important, but so is your heart." She gave Victoria a pointed look as she said the last bit. "Do not sacrifice it for some imagined duty which you think must be performed before you are five and twenty."

"I have been waiting for over ten years for my heart to gain the gentleman for whom it longs. Perhaps it is time to pack that desire away with the toys in the nursery as something from childhood that is not to accompany me into adulthood."

Diana looked truly pained at the comment. "Consider other gentlemen if you must, but do not give up on him just yet."

Victoria wove her lavender ribbon in and out between her fingers. She did not wish to lay her love for Roger aside. Indeed, she was not sure she could.

"You know he was not pleased to have Carlyle sing with you," Diana whispered. "And last evening, he did not seem happy about how much time you spent with Mr. Clayton."

Victoria tipped her head and looked at her friend. "Then, you think there is hope?"

Diana nodded.

"Very well. If you think there is hope, I shall not despair just yet." No, she would not despair. She would keep doing as she had begun yesterday. She would spend time with Mr. Clayton and a few of the other gentlemen to see if she could provoke some sort of response from Roger.

With that settled, and with only a small concern left about where Roger was, she turned her mind back to the book on her lap and the Dashwood sisters' plight as they entered London with the hopeful, matchmaking Mrs. Jennings. She wished them well, for this business of finding a husband could be a dreadful ordeal designed to crush the very soul of a lady who loved where love seemed not to be readily returned.

Chapter 9

"I will require him again in a few hours time." Roger handed the reins of his horse to a groom.

Then, as he pulled off his gloves, Roger walked behind the stable and down a small path to the pond. He tossed his gloves on the ground and removed his jacket before tossing himself under a tree. Picking up a small twig from the ground beside him, he threw it into the water. However, it did not create a very satisfying splash. With a sigh, he hauled himself up from his spot and went to gather some rocks – smooth ones which would skip across the water.

Once he had a small pile of ammunition in his hands, he returned to his place and began the task of seeing how many times he could skip each rock. Focusing on such a task and counting the hops across the pond, he hoped, would be just the sort of absorbing trivial activity which would rid his mind of the fear that had settled into it last night.

"I thought I saw you ducking behind the stables."

Roger looked up to see Diana's husband, Benjamin Berkley, approaching.

"I did not see you," Roger admitted. To be honest, he had seen very little on his ride from the Abernathy's to his home. His horse knew the way, so there was very little need to steer the animal, and so, Roger had found himself lost in his thoughts.

"I was under the impression that I was not going to see you for another week, at least," Berkley said as he sat down next to Roger.

"You aren't," Roger replied.

"And yet, here you are."

"I needed to get away from all those females." It was mostly the truth. He needed to find a place away from a *particular* female so that he could try to sort out his thoughts.

"That is understandable. How is my wife faring?"

"She seems to be enjoying herself. She has taken

a second young lady under her wing since Victoria is not challenging enough."

Berkley laughed. "That does sound like Diana. She does like a challenge, which is likely why she was willing to take me on."

Their mother had not liked Benjamin Berkley for good reason. The gentleman was not the most sedate fellow. He liked to have fun, and his fun had come in a great variety of forms before he had met Diana.

He was an excellent horseman and still found an occasional race to be something he could not resist. He had also been a great gambler at his club, though not in the usual fashion. He had not tossed away more than a few coins at a card table. Instead, he had found great delight in betting on challenges posed to him by his group of friends. One such challenge had included stealing a kiss from one of the patronesses at Almacks. He had managed to kiss the lady's cheek and, then, had found himself promptly banned from the establishment, much to his satisfaction as he claimed his winnings.

Thankfully, Diana had seemed to have a calming effect on him, for, from the time he started court- ing Roger's sister, Berkley rarely found himself act-ing rashly. And since the arrival of his son, he had become nearly decorous – nearly but not quite.

"A guinea says I can skip this rock further than you."

Roger shook his head. "I am not interested."

"Not even if I do it with my left foot against the tree. Like this." Berkley stood and placed his foot flat against the trunk of the tree at about knee height.

"You cannot skip a rock standing like that."

"I think I can," Berkley retorted.

"I am not taking your money, nor am I giving you any of mine."

"Then, let's make a different agreement. If I can skip the rock – not if I can skip it further than you, but just if I can skip it – you truly do not think I can?" he asked in response to Roger's look of disbelief.

"No, the angle is all wrong."

"You might be right, but then again, you might be wrong."

"Very well, if you can perform this feat, what do you require in payment besides my admitting that you were right?"

"You must answer one question."

"What question?" Roger eyed his brother-in-law skeptically.

"No, I will not tell you. You must agree to an unknown question, which should not be too hard to do unless, of course, you are hiding something?"

Roger tossed a rock and watched it hop three times before sinking beneath the water. There were things that he wished to keep secret, but then, if he admitted to hiding something, he knew Berkley well enough to know that the man would attempt to discover whatever it was. Roger looked at the awkward way Berkley was standing with his foot still against the tree. Surely, there was no way that he was going to be able to skip a rock.

"I accept."

"Hand me a rock. Pick the worst one for skipping."

As if Roger was planning on giving him the best rock to use for such a purpose! Roger was not unskilled at playing games of chance, and he knew that it was always best to have the odds in one's favour even if it meant arranging things to best advantage.

"You could not find a worse one?" Berkley scoffed when Roger handed him a round craggy rock that fit in his hand so that he could conceal it in a fist but only just. A large and uneven rock such as that was not for skipping — lobbing at the head of an enemy perhaps but not skipping.

"I was only doing as instructed."

Berkley shook his head. "Only because it suits your purposes," he said with a laugh.

"Precisely," Roger admitted.

"It only needs to skip once for me to win."

Roger nodded. "It is not the number of skips but the mere occurrence of, at least, one skip." His lips quirked into a smirk. "However, more than one skip would be more impressive."

Berkley's eyebrows rose as he considered that while Roger hoped the suggestion would cause him to throw the rock with too much force in the wrong direction.

"One question per skip?"

The man was proficient at twisting things. Roger shook his head.

"Very well, but I might be able to skip this more than once."

"You might," Roger agreed.

Berkley huffed, hopped his right foot into position, swung his arm out to the side, and snapped the rock into motion.

If the blasted thing did not bounce once but twice off the water! Roger shook his head. He should have known better than to enter into a bet with Berkley. There were very few challenges the man had never won, but this one had seemed such a sure loss.

Berkley removed his foot from the tree and turned with a grin to Roger. "Why are you here? And do not tell me about needing to get away from females. I want to know if it is because a particular female is chasing you and you do not wish her to do so, or if there is a particular young lady who has finally captured Roger Shelton."

Roger clenched his jaw and shook his head. He should have known that the one question Diana's husband would ask would be the one question that he did not want to answer.

"Ah ha! It is a particular young lady."

"You sound a bit like your wife," Roger grumbled.

"Well, we have been hoping for some time."

"Hoping for what? Roger asked. "That I would marry?"

Berkley nodded. "But not just marry."

Roger cocked his head and looked at his brother-in-law in confusion. "I do not follow."

Berkley shook his head. "I cannot say. I have promised."

"That does not make any sense."

"Tell me who she is. What is the name of the lady who has sent you running?"

"No, it is enough that you know there is one."

Berkley scowled. "Do I know her?" he asked as he took a seat next to where Roger was once again sitting.

"I am not telling you."

"Then, tell me why you are running away from her."

Roger drew a calming breath. How did his sister manage to endure such a persistent fellow?

"If I had to guess," Berkley said in a more serious tone, "I would say you are feeling a lot like I did when I met Diana. The thought of taking on a wife and family..." He shook his head. "Terrifying. Worse than sneaking through the fence at old Tenley's house. He had this gardener with one eye, who was a crotchety old fellow – worse than Tenley. Anyway, I survived. Neither the gardener nor his wolfhound ever caught me." He blew out a breath. "And so far, I have survived being both a husband and a father, though the thought of raising my son does still give me palpitations. However, I do not need to do it on my own. I have Diana, and she did survive having you as a brother." He nudged Roger with his elbow and chuckled.

"You are right," Roger admitted. "What do I know of responsibility?"

"Far more than you realize." Berkley shook his head. "A gentleman with a father like yours and who is still on speaking terms with that father knows more about responsibility than he might like to admit."

"I am not my father."

"None of us are. However, there is enough of him in you that you know that taking a wife is a grave responsibility. Your father is not unlike mine."

"But how do I know I can be the gentleman she deserves?"

"Do you love her?"

Roger nodded.

"Does she love you?"

That was the heart of the matter. He did not know if Victoria loved him. He shrugged.

Berkley picked up the second to last rock and sent it skittering across the pond. "Can you see her with anyone else without wishing to send that fellow to some far off desolate land to live in exile?"

"No."

Roger had wanted to physically harm Carlyle, and while he had refrained from thinking of doing away with Clayton simply because he was the brother of a good friend, Roger had wished the man would decide to leave the house party or be found in some compromising position with Miss Love so that he could not present himself as a possible suitor for Victoria.

"Then make her love you. Go back to that blasted house party and charm her out of her stockings – figuratively, not literally." He cast a sidelong grin at Roger. "Unless, of course, that helps your cause."

"As you did with Diana?"

Berkley shrugged.

"She told me," Roger admitted.

"Did she?"

"Yesterday, and I am not yet over the shock."

Berkley laughed. "You were shocked by such an admission? I highly doubt that."

"She is my sister."

"Precisely. You are not the only Shelton to have an improper bent."

Roger chuckled. "That I knew. I just did not realize it ran so deeply with my sister. And I would have been quite delighted to have remained ignorant."

Berkley laughed again. "Are you going to show your face in the house?"

"I came to retrieve a jacket."

"You could have sent a servant."

"A servant would not have been able to provoke my mother."

"You are not going to say that to her, are you?"

Roger rose as he nodded. "That is the very thing I have planned to say in response to her protest that I should not have come to retrieve that jacket."

"You mean the jacket you do not really need?"

"That is the very jacket."

"Come. You can see your nephew and take a report back to my wife about all the things she is missing."

"She cannot leave any sooner than Victoria

does," Roger said as they began their way across the lawn to the house.

"Yes, but she will be more eager to return when the party is done. And I am very eager to have her return." He drew and released a deep breath. It was a sound of longing — one which Roger's heart felt and understood.

"I am likely going to run afoul of my wife and possibly Miss Hamilton, but..." Berkley stopped speaking and looked as if he were not certain he should continue. "However, if the lady who has captured your heart is the one whom Diana and I hope you will finally notice, then, I feel I must, as a service to my fellow man and brother, relieve some of your anxiety and tell you that I do not think your suit would be refused."

Roger's brow furrowed. Was the fellow speaking about Victoria? Was that why he might find her put out with him for having spoken to Roger?

"I can say no more than this." Berkley looked around the garden before leaning a bit closer to Roger and whispering, "she has loved you for years."

Roger stood stalk still. "Victoria?"

Grinning, Berkley clapped Roger on the shoulder. "You did not hear that from me. I will deny it vehemently. Now, come along. We have a child to see and an imaginary jacket to retrieve."

"Victoria loves me?"

"Why do you suppose she has not yet married?" Berkley gave Roger a shove to start him walking.

It was an action for which Roger was grateful, for it was as if his brain could not think of anything but those three words *Victoria loved him*.

"Is that truly why she has not married?" Roger asked when his mind was able to conquer things such as walking and speaking.

"You did not hear that from me either," Berkley said as he opened the door to the servant's entrance. "I will deny it vehemently."

Chapter 10

The evening breeze stirred the curtains in the drawing room. Dinner was over, and the card tables were being set up. From the chair where Victoria sat, she could see Grace and her sister, Felicity, standing on the lawn talking with Mr. Clayton and Mr. Ramsey. Grace's features were all animation as she attended to the conversation.

Oh, to be young and hopeful. Victoria remembered the excitement she had felt during her first season. Every event was new. Every gentleman was a possibility – well, not an actual possibility for her heart was already lost to her friend – but an imagined one. And there had been the ever-present hope that some new dress or hairstyle would be the one which would finally capture Roger's attention.

Victoria turned her eyes back to the room. Roger

had still not returned from wherever he had gone. There had been much-whispered speculation at dinner. Some thought he had bored of the party and left. Others thought perhaps he had been asked to leave after some indiscretion – not that they had heard of any particular reckless behaviour, but he did have a reputation for dalliances. At least one lady had sighed wishing that she was the cause for his removal from the party.

"It is far too excellent an evening to spend inside, Miss Hamilton." Mr. Carlyle stood before her. "Would you be so kind as to allow me to walk with you around the garden?"

"I had not thought to move from my chair until required to play a hand of some game," Victoria replied with a smile. She would not be opposed to a walk in the garden with Diana or Grace or even Mr. Clayton, but she had no desire to encourage Mr. Carlyle.

"I promise we will not go far. Just to the rotunda and back."

"My chaperone is not here to accompany me."

"We will be in the open. No one would frown on us for walking side by side in clear view of everyone."

"But I really should let Mrs. Berkley know where I am."

"I saw her not two minutes ago standing in the garden, just outside the door, speaking with Mrs. Love."

Victoria glanced out the window. The rotunda was not all that far from the house, and there were no trees or bushes to obstruct the view. "Very well. I shall walk with you, but only after I have informed Mrs. Berkley and asked her if she would like to join us."

She placed her hand in his outstretched one and allowed him to first assist her in rising and then to escort her to where Diana was speaking with Mrs. Love.

"Mrs. Berkley," Carlyle began when the ladies had paused their conversation and looked his direction, "Miss Hamilton has given me permission to escort her to the rotunda and back if you will allow it."

Diana gave Victoria a questioning look.

"I thought you might like to join us," Victoria said.

"Oh, if you are wanting company, Felicity is a great walker," Mrs. Love inserted. She stepped away from them slightly and called, "Felicity," while waving her handkerchief.

Victoria's smile tightened on her lips so that she did not visibly cringe at the action.

"We older ladies would much rather sit or stand and watch you younger ladies, would we not, Mrs. Berkley?"

Before Diana could do more than open her mouth to speak, Mrs. Love was once again calling to her daughter.

"It would be such a fine thing for a group of young ladies and gentlemen to walk without us. Oh, good," she said as her daughter approached. "Felicity dear, Mr. Carlyle and Miss Hamilton are looking for people to join them on a walk to the rotunda, and, knowing how fond you are of walking, I naturally suggested you would be delighted to join them."

Felicity looked from her mother to Mr. Carlyle and then to Victoria. She smiled at Mr. Carlyle, but, when she looked at Victoria, she raised a brow as if she wondered why Mr. Carlyle would wish to walk with her. "Of course, I would be pleased to join you, Mr. Carlyle." She batted her lashes.

"Did I not say she would be happy to join you?" Mrs. Love beamed at her daughter.

"I shall return with an escort," Felicity said before hurrying back to her sister and the two gentlemen she had been talking to before her mother had called her.

"If I know my Felicity, you will also be joined by Grace as well as Mr. Ramsey and Mr. Clayton. Felicity does seem to be a favourite amongst the gentlemen," Mrs. Love whispered before tittering behind her fan and declaring that such a thing was entirely too improper to say, but a mother could not help her delight at seeing a daughter so well-received. She placed a hand on Diana's arm and added, "The number of soirees to which we had invitations during this past season was nearly overwhelming. She was very popular."

"How fortunate for you," Diana said.

"Are you certain you do not wish to walk with us?" Victoria asked Diana.

"Oh, you are too kind, Miss Hamilton, but we shall take our ease on that bench over there until you return," Mrs. Love answered, causing Diana to scowl briefly.

"I think Mrs. Love desires my presence," Diana answered.

"It does seem that way," Victoria agreed softly.

"And I suppose I would like to be close to the house and easily found should my brother return," Diana added.

"Oh," Mrs. Love said in an eager whisper, "I should like to know the true reason for his disappearance."

She was not alone in that wish. Victoria wanted to know the same thing. However, Victoria was not the sort of lady to say such a thing in front of others. If she and Diana had been alone, she would have said the same thing, but seeing as they were not, she held her tongue, which seemed to be a skill Mrs. Love seemed not to possess. How Grace had grown into the sweet, though naïve, young woman she was still baffled Victoria. She could see where Grace got her fondness for filling the air with a constant stream of words, but neither Mrs. Love nor Felicity seemed to possess the sweetness that Grace had.

"Did I not tell you?" Mrs. Love said with no little amount of excitement as Felicity approached.

Victoria caught herself before her eyebrows

could rise in surprise for Felicity did not have her hand on Mr. Clayton's arm but rather on Mr. Ramsey's.

"Mr. Carlyle, we are all ready to proceed to the rotunda," Felicity declared.

Victoria caught Grace's eyes and sent her a questioning look. Grace shrugged one shoulder and smiled a sad half-smile, while Mr. Clayton looked resigned.

The poor man was not only being thrown over but in a very open and grand fashion. She would have to speak to Roger. Mr. Clayton needed to find someone other than Miss Love to court. No amount of beauty was worth being treated poorly! Why the gentleman would do much better to pursue Miss Grace!

It had been said in jest when they were all gathered on the lawn yesterday, but as Victoria considered it now, it was not a deplorable idea other than it would mean Mr. Clayton would have to see Miss Love on a regular basis. That was not something Victoria would be able to countenance, and she imagined it must be the same for gentlemen. How did anyone, regardless of gender, watch the person whom they thought they had loved – or perchance did love and still loved – happily attach themselves to another without losing their equanimity.

"I apologize. I was woolgathering," Victoria said when she realized Mr. Carlyle had asked her a question.

"I was merely wondering if you were fond of walking."

"Oh, yes. I rather like it."

"Do you have a particular path that you walk when you are at home? I know I tend to ride in the same direction each morning unless I make a conscious choice to take a different route," Mr. Carlyle said.

"Does that mean you prefer riding to walking?"

"I must admit that I do. There is nothing quite like feeling the rush of the wind and the power of the beast on which you are seated when the horse is thundering along some field."

"I would have to agree. That is a very intoxicating feeling."

Mr. Carlyle looked at her in surprise. "You allow your horse to gallop?"

Victoria nodded. "Trotting is no way to win a race."

Her companion looked taken aback by such information. "You race?"

"Occasionally, yes."

His lips turned downward as a startled, yet curious expression settled on his face. "Neither of my sisters will allow their horses to do more than trot. They claim it is far too dangerous and unladylike."

Unladylike? While Victoria would like to take exception to being referred to as unladylike, she paused and considered that being thought so by a gentleman like Mr. Carlyle might not be so bad a thing. It might just stop him from pursuing her at all, which would please not only Victoria but also Felicity if the way she kept looking over her shoulder at Victoria was any indication.

"Dangerous or no, I still maintain it is the only way to win a race."

"I am not certain I have met a lady who races horses," Mr. Carlyle muttered.

Or perhaps, he had just not met any who would admit to racing.

"But we were speaking of walking, were we not? Before I was distracted by your preference for riding," Victoria said.

"Yes, yes, we were. I believe I had inquired if there was a particular path you favoured."

"There is," Victoria replied with a nod. "But I must say it is not actually at my home. It is at Mr. Shelton's. We are neighbors, and our parents are good friends," she explained, not that she thought Mr. Carlyle did not already know that — no matter what sort of feigned look of surprise he wore. "On their estate, there is a path that winds down from the stables to a frog pond and then through a small stand of trees before opening into a sheep's pasture. It is not a very long walk, but it has such a variety of scenery that makes it most enjoyable. And, if one wishes, a stop at the pond to listen to the frogs is..." she sighed, "peaceful. Absolutely peaceful."

"It sounds charming. Do you walk there alone?" There was a particular tone to his question that hinted at wishing to know if Roger were a rival.

"Not always," Victoria replied. "Over the years, I have, at times, walked there with Mrs. Berkley – though less after she married than before, of course – and when Mr. Shelton is home, he will, on occasion accompany me." And capture at least one frog whom he would address as Mr. Brown and ask him how he had been keeping himself and if he still attended tea parties. Her lips tipped up at the thought. Roger would be an excellent father. His children would never want for entertainment. She caught a sigh before it escaped her as she considered that she might have to watch him entertain children who were not hers.

"And do you visit your neighbors often?"

Victoria nodded. "My parents and the Sheltons are great friends. We are in each other's company to some degree several times a week. My mother will call on Mrs. Shelton, or Mrs. Shelton will call on my mother. And when Diana and I were young, we spent a great deal of time playing together and being tormented by her brother."

"Then, Mrs. Berkley is very nearly like a sister to you and Mr. Shelton, a brother."

Victoria smiled. "Nearly." But not quite. Mrs. Berkley might be a sister, but Roger was not a brother. He was her friend, her very dear friend, who had captured her heart.

"Oh!" Felicity cried. "There was a rock. Oh, dear! My ankle turned." She limped on her left foot and leaned heavily on Mr. Ramsey's arm, pressing herself against him as she did so.

"You should sit down," Mr. Clayton said. "It is a fortunate thing we have reached the rotunda."

"Indeed, it is!" Felicity agreed. "Would you help me take a seat on the steps?" She asked Mr. Ramsey.

Mr. Ramsey eagerly assisted her.

Felicity held her foot out in front of her and twirled it this way and that while whimpering softly.

"This is very unfortunate!" Grace declared. "I heard Mrs. Abernathy just today speaking to Mama about the ball she is planning, and you love to dance."

"Oh!" Felicity brightened. "I am certain my ankle shall be well by then."

"If it is not, I shall dance with every gentleman for you," Grace volunteered as she crouched down to rub her sister's ankle.

Felicity's lips curled slightly as if displeased before she turned her look of disdain into a grimace. "Do be careful, Grace. And I am certain that with just a bit of rest, I shall be able to dance every dance."

"If you are not able to dance, there is always the chance of a stroll in the garden," Mr. Carlyle said.

Felicity ducked her head and blushed but not before Victoria saw her cast an uneasy glance at Mr. Clayton. "I do enjoy gardens."

"Indeed," Mr. Clayton muttered. He turned and looked back towards the house. "They will likely start playing games soon. We should head back."

"But I had hoped to see the far side of the rotunda," Felicity said with a small pout.

"You do not need me for that," Mr. Clayton said. "I find I have had my fill of *gardens*."

Victoria's eyebrows rose. It appeared Mr. Clayton had reached his limit for endurance. She could not help but feel somewhat happy for him.

"Do you wish to return to the house, or will you stay with your sister?" Mr. Clayton asked Grace.

"Umm," Grace looked uneasily at her sister. "It would be rather unkind to make Mr. Clayton return to the house by himself."

"Then you must accompany him," Felicity said. "I am certain Mr. Carlyle and Mr. Ramsey will see me safely returned. My ankle is feeling much better already. I think it was only a small turn and likely will only bruise with no other ill effects." She straightened, lowered her foot to the ground and held a hand out to Mr. Ramsey to help her rise. "Do not tell mother I have hurt myself. I would not wish for her to worry."

"Oh, goodness no! Of course, I would not wish for her to worry either."

And with that, Grace took Mr. Clayton's arm, and they left Victoria precisely where she did not wish to be — at the rotunda with Felicity, Mr. Ramsey, and Mr. Carlyle.

Chapter 11

Roger slipped into the Abernathy's library and made his way to the liquor cabinet. A bottle of port stood at the ready surrounded by several glasses.

For the past two nights, several of the gentlemen in attendance had claimed the library as a haven of sorts where they could escape the festivities in other portions of the house.

"There is a bet going on about you."

Roger turned from the sideboard, carafe of port still in hand, and eyed Mr. Yardley, the only other gentleman in the room. "About my absence?'

Mr. Yardley nodded as he rose to join Roger. "Apparently, some did not expect you to return." He handed his empty glass to Roger to be refilled. "I would not have returned," Yardley muttered. "Blasted house parties were designed to torture us, gentlemen. I am certain of it. I have five sisters at home. I do not need to be sent to a house brimming with young debutantes to let me know I need to marry. Between my sisters and my mother, I have constant reminders."

He picked up his glass. "However, I would like to have all five of my sisters here so I could see them married off. Then, I could find a quiet place to ruminate at least once during the day."

"So you would not be interested in a wife who has a talent for talking?" Roger asked.

Yardley snorted. "Heavens, no!"

"I imagine that once they are all married, you will be able to take the place of your sisters for your mother then?"

The man peered over his glass at Roger, his brow furrowed. "How do you mean?"

"I assume your mother is used to having five females with whom to converse, is she not?" Roger unbuttoned his jacket and relaxed into a chair across from Yardley. The man was one of the gents Grace had listed, and since the man was used to talkative women, perhaps he might be amenable to considering Grace – with a little persuasion.

Yardley nodded. "Go on."

"When all your sisters are finally married off – are they younger or older?"

"The youngest is just turned fifteen."

"Well, then, it will not be long until all of them are married, I would imagine."

"I would hope," Yardley muttered into his glass before taking a gulp of its contents.

"And when they are all settled at estates which are likely too far away for daily visits, your mother will need someone with whom to discuss fashion and recipes and the like. Of course, she might have enough neighbours to suffice, and you will be left to yourself." Roger bit back a smile at the look of horror on Yardley's face. "Not many neighbours?"

"Only three, and they are worse than my sisters for gossip!"

"I suppose a quiet wife would be willing to listen to your mother and likely agree to everything she says."

The look of horror on the face of the gentleman across from Roger deepened.

"Or," Roger swirled his drink, "you could choose a wife who is not so very quiet but is sweet and likely to question things. I would imagine such a lady would spend a great deal of time keeping your mother occupied, but, well, there is no way around it, you would still be subjected to a degree of chatter. However, the volume of two ladies cannot be as great as six."

Yardley drained his glass and placed it, with a loud thud, on a table he could reach from his chair. "And do you have a particular lady in mind who fits these qualifications?"

Roger took a slow sip of his port. "Perhaps. Is your mother kind?"

"Exceptionally."

"Are you opposed to a young wife?"

"First season?"

Roger inclined his head in an affirmative response. "Soon to enter her second."

Yardley's brow furrowed while he scratched his jaw.

"You are not so very old," Roger prompted. "You are what? A year older than me?"

Yardley shrugged. "Twenty-seven."

"The same age then."

"Does she have feathers for brains like so many do?"

Roger shook his head. "She does not seem to

be excessively bright, but she has potential for growth."

"So she wants guidance?"

Roger nodded. For all that Grace thought she was well-accomplished, she had spent too long in her sister's shadow to have learned anything of real value. Oh, she had no doubt learned to flirt and speak about inanely trivial things, but he sincerely doubted that she had learned how to think for herself. Simply being removed from her sister's influence would be a boon to her.

"Who?" Yardley demanded.

"Miss Grace Love."

For a moment, Roger thought Yardley's eyes might pop out of his head.

"That coquette? Does Clayton not want her?"

Roger placed his glass alongside Yardley's. "No, no, that is Miss Felicity Love. I would take a wide berth around that one, and Clayton would do well to be rid of her. Grace is her sister."

Yardley's brows were still lifted as he shook his head.

"They are as alike as a rainy day and a sunny morning," Roger assured Yardley. "I dare say that

Miss Grace received all the sweetness in that family while her sister got none."

Yardley still did not look convinced that he should consider Grace.

"She will likely not thank me for this, but Miss Grace has mentioned that she finds you attractive. Therefore, persuading her to accept an offer should not be too challenging should you think, after getting to know her, that you would rub along well together. She is no pauper."

"I had heard that," Yardley muttered. "Carlyle and Ramsey mentioned it in relation to the elder Love chit. Both are looking to make improvements to their estates."

"And you? Are you looking to improve your estate?"

Yardley shook his head. "I am looking for someone to be the mother of the heir to my estate."

The right corner of Roger's lips tipped into a sly smirk. "It would be no hardship to attempt such a thing with Miss Grace. She is not so thin as some and perhaps a trifle shorter than I might prefer, but she is not without some very pleasing curves."

Yardley chuckled. "And, from what I hear, you are well-versed in such things."

"Was," Roger said. He had noticed the fine figures of several ladies in attendance, but not one of them had appealed to him as they once would have. To be honest, for some time now, he had not found as much enjoyment in studying the female form as he used to. He had pondered that thought for a while as he sat in his room discussing marriage and family with Berkley, and, on his ride back to the Abernathys', he had come to understand that it was because he craved something more. *Someone* more. He did not just want a pretty lady to charm and seduce. He wanted a friend – a most beloved friend. Someone who would not only warm his bed but who would also tease him out of a bad humour and encourage – and even scold – him to making wise choices.

"Why do you not pursue her if you think she is so tempting and sweet-tempered?"

Roger shook his head. "My desires lie elsewhere."

"Miss Hamilton?"

"Yes." There was no point in denying it, for he intended to make his preference known as soon as he could find a few moments alone with his friend. He pulled at his left sleeve. He knew that Berkley had told him Victoria was favourably inclined towards him, but still the thought of presenting himself to her in such a way made him uneasy. She deserved so much better than he had ever been. However, in his mind, there was no man in the world who was truly good enough for her, and so, it was just as well that he present himself to her rather than some other undeserving fool.

"I had thought so," Yardley cried. "That is why I put my money on you returning – especially with Carlyle sniffing around her purse strings."

Roger tipped his head and studied Yardley. "I beg your pardon?"

"I told you. Carlyle wishes to improve his estate, and everyone knows Miss Hamilton has the heaviest purse."

Was that the reason the fellow was pursuing Victoria?

"Miss Abernathy is just as well-dowered," Roger said.

"But Miss Abernathy is a trifle more difficult to pry away from her mother's side long enough to *convince* her that she should marry him."

Roger's heart hammered in his ears. "What do you mean?"

Yardley chuckled. "Surely, someone with your reputation must know how one goes about persuading a lady."

But this was Victoria. She was not some lady. She was... Victoria. He rose. It was perhaps best if he showed his face tonight rather than waiting until morning as he had thought to do.

"They are playing cards in the drawing room," Yardley offered as Roger reached the door.

"Do you wish to play and perhaps observe Miss Grace?" Roger asked.

"No, I would like to stay right where I am in undisturbed bliss and most likely getting properly foxed."

Roger pulled the door open to find the very young lady about whom he had been talking standing in the hall with Everett, attempting to persuade him to play cards.

"You have returned!" she cried in delight when she saw him.

"Indeed, I have, Miss Grace," he said as he cast a significant look at Yardley, but Yardley only shook his head and remained seated where he was.

"Is there alcohol in there?" Clayton asked.

Roger moved out of his way and allowed him to enter the library.

"My sister has been abominably rude," Grace whispered. "And I think he is giving her up," she added after taking a peek inside the library.

"Is he?" That seemed a development of no little significance, and Roger could understand why Everett was in search of some libation. Were Roger not in desperate need of finding Victoria, he would take himself back into the library and attempt to help the fellow through it with a few encouraging words and by refilling his glass as needed.

Grace nodded as she poked her head around Roger so that she could see inside the library again. "Mr. Clayton," she said, "please do not drink too much. You will only feel dreadful in the morning."

"I will only drink as much as is needed," he assured, lifting his glass in salute to her words.

She marched into the room and added in a low voice. "She is not worth casting up your accounts and feeling as if a battalion of soldiers is using your head for their parade. Oh, good evening, Mr. Yardley. Are you not going to play cards?"

He shook his head.

"And do you have as good an excuse as Mr. Clayton?"

Yardley opened his mouth and then closed it.

"He does not," Roger said, earning a glare from Yardley.

Grace's brow furrowed and her lips puckered. "Are you a bore, Mr. Yardley?"

"A bore?" he cried. "I should think not. I am a rather interesting fellow."

Grace shook her head and sighed. "I am afraid that is not true, for all the interesting gentlemen are playing cards – save, of course, for those who have been treated very poorly by my sister."

"There is no chaperone in here," Roger warned.

"Oh, goodness!" Grace cried and scampered to the door. "I forgot in my concern for Mr. Clayton. You do not suppose I am ruined now, do you? That would be quite horrid."

"I am absolutely certain your reputation is still intact," Roger replied with a chuckle. "And if it is not, I am sure one of us gentlemen would do right by you."

Grace shook her head. "Not you. Your sister told me. You will not be tricked into marrying no matter what might happen to a lady's reputation because of her scheming." Her brow furrowed. "Of course, I was not scheming. I did not mean to trick anyone into marriage."

"I am certain you did not," Roger assured her as he closed the door to the library.

"It is not that I would not consider it, which is likely not right for me to do, is it?"

"No, it is not. Or I imagine that is what my sister would say." Roger offered her his arm, and they began walking toward the drawing room.

Grace glanced back over her shoulder. "Mr. Yardley is very handsome, is he not?"

"I suppose he must be if you say so," Roger replied.

"And poor Mr. Clayton." She sighed. "I quite like him. I did from the time we arrived at Heathcote. However, as Felicity pointed out, she is older, and so it is she who should marry first."

Roger stopped walking. "And you gave him up for her?"

Grace shrugged. "I had not lost my heart to him." She glanced back at the library door. "And I thought my sister had." She shook her head. "But apparently, she has not, for she is at the rotunda with Mr. Ramsey likely letting him kiss her."

"But I thought you thought Mr. Ramsey was of interest."

Again, Grace shrugged. "I did, but..."

"Your sister is older?"

Grace nodded.

"She deserves to be an old maid," Roger muttered. "Is she at the rotunda alone with Mr. Ramsey?"

"No. Miss Hamilton and Mr. Carlyle are with them."

Roger pulled Grace across the drawing room in his hurry to reach the window. "I do not see them."

"That is because Felicity wished to see the far side of the rotunda." She blew out a breath. "So she can kiss him," she added in a disappointed whisper.

"Do you wish to go to the rotunda with me?" Roger asked.

"Why are you going there?" Grace hurried behind him toward the garden door.

"Because I am not going to allow Mr. Carlyle to kiss Victoria."

Grace blinked. "Do you think he will?"

Unfortunately, Roger did. The backside of the rotunda was the perfect secluded place for a gentleman to attempt a seduction. He stopped just out-side the garden door and pulled Grace off the path. "Do you remember how we were talking about finding a match for Miss Hamilton?"

Grace nodded.

"And can you keep a secret?"

Again, Grace nodded.

"I have found her a match."

"You have? Who? Is it Mr. Yardley?'

Roger blew out a breath as he shook his head. "It is me. She is the one who I fear losing more than I fear losing my freedom."

"Oh, that is the most delightful thing!"

There was no mistaking Grace's delight for it was evident in her excited whisper and the quick clap of her hands as well as the smile on her face.

"Then, we must hurry," she said as she took his arm and stepped back onto the garden path.

Chapter 12

The evening breeze ruffled the hem of Victoria's dress. It was a pleasant enough evening to be out in the garden, or it would be if she had been in the garden with anyone other than her current companions. She glanced back at the house one last time before following Felicity around the rotunda.

"Oh, a path!" Felicity cried.

There before them was a narrow path that wound down the hill and into some trees.

"Would you like to see where it leads?" Mr. Ramsey asked.

"No," Victoria replied before Felicity could say a word. "We are to return to play games. Your mother will be worried, as will Mrs. Berkley."

Felicity rolled her eyes and giggled. "You do not need to accompany us. You may stay right here with Mr. Carlyle. I am certain he would not feel it an inconvenience to wait here with you while Mr. Ramsey and I explore this little path. I am sure it would not take long."

"No longer than necessary," Mr. Ramsey said with a wink for Felicity, who blushed and ducked her head while peeking up at the gentleman at her side.

"I am not allowing you to go wandering down a path with no chaperone." Victoria held Felicity's gaze.

"You are such a prude." Felicity smirked at Mr. Ramsey. "Whatever do you expect us to do while we are out of your sight?"

"It is most improper, and I shall not be a party to your ruin."

"What Miss Hamilton says is true," Mr. Carlyle said. "It would not be right for us to allow either of you to play so recklessly with Miss Love's reputation." He turned to Victoria. "I think we ought to accompany them."

"We are expected back. We told our chaperones that we were going to the rotunda and back."

"And we are at the rotunda," Mr. Carlyle replied, "and when we return, we will be back. I see no untruth in what we said even if we take a short stroll down this path."

Victoria gaped at him. He saw nothing untrue in his story? "To the rotunda and back did not include to the rotunda and then a little further and back." She folded her arms and glared, in turn, at each of the others who were with her.

"Then, we have no option but to wait here for them to return."

"We have the option of them not taking a walk down that path." Victoria pointed to the path down which Felicity and Mr. Ramsey were already walking. "Of all the deviant and deceitful things!"

"There is no harm done," Mr. Carlyle cajoled. "We can still see them."

"And when they reach the trees, Mr. Carlyle, then what?"

Victoria descended to the path. She shook her head and huffed attempting to clear some of the anger she felt at being placed in the situation in which she found herself. Miss Love was horrid. Simply and utterly horrid. There was no other word for her. She treated her sister poorly and ignored the gentleman who was courting her while blatantly flirting with another. And then there was

Mr. Carlyle who saw nothing wrong with what was being done?

"I promise you that I shall never agree to walk with you in the garden again," she said, allowing her displeasure to bubble over.

"Not even when we marry?"

Victoria stood stalk still and turned slowly toward Mr. Carlyle. "I beg your pardon?" She was certain her ears must be playing tricks with her mind. He certainly could not be presuming that she would marry him!

"I was only wondering if your never walking with me again was to be confined to this house party or if it extended to when we were married."

She had heard him correctly. "We are not marrying."

He smiled. "I think we are. We are quite good together. Your piano playing mixes well with my singing. You are lively and thoughtful – just what I prefer in a lady."

"Piano playing and liveliness? These are the requirements for your wife?"

"They are but two."

"No." She shook her head to emphasize her point. "No, I will not marry you."

He caught her hand. "Please, Miss Hamilton? I can give you more reasons if you give me time to consider them, but surely, you feel the attraction between us."

He was mad. That must be it. There was no attraction between them. She merely tolerated him because she had not wished to be rude.

He lifted her fingers to his lips.

"Mr. Carlyle, I will thank you to unhand me this instant. I feel nothing akin to attraction to you, and I have no desire to marry you."

He dropped her hand and shrugged. "What will the others say?"

Disquiet settled around her chest, pulling it tightly in on itself, forcing out what breath she held in her lungs. "What will who say?"

He waved his hand back toward the house. "The others." His lips tipped up on the right side. "We have lost sight of Miss Love and Mr. Ramsey, and they have lost sight of us."

"You would lie?"

His brow furrowed though his smile did not fade. "Lie? About what?"

She looked down the path toward where Felicity should be but was not. Then, she turned toward her companion, dipped a curtsey, and said, "Good evening, Mr. Carlyle," before heading back toward the rotunda. She needed to be back in the safety of the house. She cared not what happened to Felicity at the moment. The girl had made her decision, and she could face the consequences. Victoria was not prepared to be forced into marrying Mr. Carlyle.

"Miss Hamilton," he called after her, "the damage is already done, do you not think?"

She stopped at the top of the steps to the rotunda. Looking down at him where he stood on the ground below her, she shook her head. "Damage or no damage. I will not marry you, Mr. Carlyle." She held up her hand as he began to ascend the stairs. "No, Mr. Carlyle, you must remain here in case, Mr. Ramsey cannot carry Miss Love to the house by himself."

His brow furrowed. "I do not understand your meaning."

"Her ankle."

"It is not injured."

"Oh, I am certain you are quite correct about that." The little vixen had been walking far too quickly down that path for her ankle to have been even slightly injured. It was a ploy. Nothing more. An act to rid herself of Mr. Clayton and her sister so that she could have Mr. Ramsey all to herself.

"However," Victoria continued, "she did say it was injured, and I feel it is only proper that I seek help for her."

"But, she does not wish to worry her mother."

Victoria laughed. "Of course, she does not, for that would not give her the opportunity she is now taking to be alone with Mr. Ramsey, and, I am certain, Mr. Ramsey is happy to help with any subterfuge that would lead him to where he is now, doing what he is likely doing." She smiled at Mr. Carlyle's surprised expression. "I have been friends with Mr. Shelton for far too long not to know how these assignations go."

"Indeed?" Mr. Carlyle's brows rose before a smirk crawled across his lips. "And how precisely do you know?"

Victoria's cheeks flamed at his insinuation. "It is not how you imagine. He merely likes to shock me with stories." That was probably not helping her cause. "It matters not. You must stay here, and I will inform Mrs. Love of her daughter's injury."

She spun on her heels and hurried around the rotunda.

She should not have been hurrying quite so quickly, for it was her haste which made her lose her footing on the bottom step of the rotunda.

She brushed the dirt from her palms. They would likely bruise, but the skin was not broken, no matter how much the stinging wanted her to believe it was. Her dress, however, was not so fortunate. There was a small tear at the bottom where her foot had caught it as she had risen from the ground after falling. She sighed as she noticed there was also a green stain from the grass on her left hip.

She dashed a tear from her cheek. This was nothing about which to cry. A little pain was not worth the tears. However, returning to the house as she was would be worth a few tears if Mr. Carlyle chose to tell tales, for those tales would be much easier to believe when coupled with the state of her clothing.

She would take the less direct path to the house. The one that would take her to the side where she could then slip around to the front. It would be easier to sneak in and up to her room without being seen if she approached it in such a fashion.

Oh! Her knee hurt, but she was not about to lift her skirt to check it until she had gained the privacy of her room.

Thankfully, the only person near the front of the house when she entered was Mr. Clayton, who was making his way up the grand staircase with a rather full glass of what appeared to be port in his hand.

"Miss Hamilton," he greeted as she made to pass him.

"Mr. Clayton."

"Your dress is looking worse for the wear."

"As are you," she returned with a smile. His cheeks were flushed, and his gaze wandered, and if Victoria were to guess based on how her brother looked when he had indulged too much in alcohol, Mr. Clayton was well on his way to being foxed.

He chuckled. "I am not feeling it, though I suspect I will tomorrow, and it will make for a long ride home."

"You are leaving?"

He nodded. "It seems best. Miss Love is off in the garden with Mr. Ramsey."

"Yes, I know."

He blew out a breath and offered her his arm. She thought about not taking it until he swayed. Then, she considered how taking his arm was a good way to ensure his safe arrival to the hall above them.

"You will be missed," she said as she helped him up the stairs.

He snorted. "Not by many. House parties." He shook his head. "Dreadful things."

"Indeed." Victoria could not agree more with his assessment.

"No need to stay where I am not welcome," he added.

Victoria pointed him in the direction of his room and stood at the top of the stairs watching for a few minutes to make sure he was far away from any danger of falling down the stairs before she turned and went to her room, where she sat on her bed and examined her somewhat bloody knee.

She had to agree with Mr. Clayton — going home did not seem so bad an idea.

She rose and rang the bell for her maid before going to the washstand to pour a little water into the basin for washing her hands.

"Would you send for Mrs. Berkley," she said

when her maid entered. "And then I think I shall retire for the evening."

"Right away, miss."

Victoria removed her shoes and pulled off her stockings. They were dirty and torn but not beyond repair. Once her knee had been washed, she began the work of undoing her hair while she waited for her maid to return and help her with the unfastening of her dress.

"Blast," she muttered. She had put Roger's lavender ribbon in her hair tonight in case he came back. She had foolishly thought that if he saw it, he might realize how much she cared for him. And now, that ribbon was missing. It had likely fallen out when she fell. She should have woven it into her hair rather than just using it as an adornment on her comb.

"Is something wrong?" Diana asked as she came into the room.

"I fell," Victoria turned so Diana could see her knee.

"Oh, my dear, how did that happen?"

"I was attempting to get away from Mr. Carlyle as quickly as I could." She shrugged. "I should have been more careful."

Diana wore a horrified expression as she crossed to where Victoria sat. "What happened?"

Victoria shook her head. "I will tell you, but not now. Right now, I need you to tell Mrs. Love that her eldest daughter has sneaked away down a secluded path behind the rotunda with Mr. Ramsey. She twisted her ankle earlier, and so Mr. Carlyle was good enough to stay in case there was a need for his assistance in returning her to the house."

The eyebrow over Diana's left eye rose. "Mr. Carlyle was good enough to do that?"

"That is what you are to tell Mrs. Love."

"And then, you will tell me all?"

Victoria nodded. She would gladly tell her friend all that there was to tell, after which she would ask Diana to take her home.

Diana gave her one more concerned look before exiting the room and leaving Victoria to the care of her maid.

Chapter 13

"Where is Victoria?" Roger demanded.

Three people were descending the steps to the rotunda when Grace and Roger reached it, and not one of them was Victoria.

"Victoria is it?" Carlyle smirked.

Roger glowered at him. "We have been friends our whole lives. Now, where is she? Miss Grace said she was here."

He was not opposed to hitting a popinjay such as Carlyle if needed. In fact, he'd be rather pleased to do it. However, now was not the time for such things no matter in which direction his feelings ran on the subject.

"Oh, she was. I assure you she was." Grace clutched his arm more tightly. "She was right here when I left."

"I do not doubt you," Roger assured her. "What

is that?" he asked as, out of the corner of his eye, he noticed Miss Love stooping to pick something up off the ground.

"My, you are a suspicious fellow this evening, Mr. Shelton." Miss Love spoke in a sweet, teasing tone; however, Roger was not in the frame of mind to politely endure teasing. He rarely was when the source was a conniving female such as Miss Love.

"And your cheeks are rather flushed, and you have a few tendrils of hair out of place." He added a smile and fluttered his lashes much as she had done a moment ago. He chuckled when she gasped as if affronted. "That will not convince me of your innocence. I know full-well the advantage that a secluded location such as the far side of the rotunda and the path beyond can give to those who are hoping to avoid propriety for a few minutes."

"There is a path behind the rotunda?" Grace asked, leaning her head to the side as if attempting to look around the stone building in front of them. "How do you know?"

"I have seen it," Roger answered. "I always make myself familiar with all potential traps and routes of escape," he added. "I do not intend to marry until I decide to marry."

"To avoid a trap?" Carlyle said with a laugh. "Do you not mean devise a plan to take advantage of the seclusion such a spot affords?"

Roger affected a nonchalant shrug. "Not unlike what you and Ramsey were about."

"We were only seeing the other side of the rotunda," Carlyle assured him with a hint of anger in his voice.

"Yes, well, a seduction is much more effective if there is a lady to seduce," Roger quipped, causing the gentleman's eyes to narrow. Drawing out Carlyle could be an exceptionally satisfying prospect.

"I was not alone," Carlyle replied. "Miss Hamilton was willing to keep me company."

He felt Grace grasp at his arm, as he moved to close the distance between himself and Carlyle. "Where. Is. She?" He enunciated each word slowly.

"She returned to the house," Ramsey put forward.

"Yes, yes," Carlyle agreed. "But not until *after* she informed me of how well you have taught her about assignations."

As much as Roger wished to hit the man, he

refrained, allowing himself to only give Carlyle a good shove that sent him stumbling backward. "She is a good friend. I would be careful how I spoke of her if I were you."

"Is that so?" Carlyle taunted. "Exactly how good a friend is she, Shelton? We all know your reputation with the fairer sex."

"Mr. Shelton." Grace was at his elbow. "Please, do not hit him."

"Why not?" He pulled his arm away from her. "Even you must know what he is insinuating about Victoria."

"I do, and it is most improper. But think of the explanation that will be required if Mr. Carlyle returns with a black eye or bloody nose." She looked at Carlyle and added, "Not that he does not deserve both."

From the vehement tone she used to say that last bit, it appeared to Roger that there was some fire hidden within Miss Grace Love. Hopefully, she would learn to use that fire when dealing with her sister, who was smiling behind her fingers as if what was happening was the most amusing things she had ever witnessed.

"Do you find me entertaining, Miss Love?"

Roger asked. "Or do you find it diverting when someone accuses another lady of impropriety?"

Felicity gasped. "You are very forward, Mr. Shelton."

"And you are a conniving wench, Miss Love."

"Mr. Shelton!" Grace scolded.

"She is. You have seen how she has treated Mr. Clayton."

Grace shrugged and nodded.

"Mr. Clayton, who," he glared at Felicity, "happens to be the brother of my very dear friend."

"It was not right what she did," Miss Grace said.

"Indeed, it was not. You are far more sensible than your sister will likely ever be, Miss Grace. Shall we return to the house?" Spending any further time with Ramsey, Carlyle, and Miss Love seemed a poor idea for it would only lead to him being less and less able to rein in his temper and would do nothing to help him find Victoria.

"Mr. Ramsey is not good enough for you," he whispered as he and Grace began to walk back to the house. "You deserve far better."

"Thank you," Grace muttered sadly.

They walked silently for a few moments, and with every step, Roger became more and more indigent about whatever had transpired at the rotunda – and not just because of what Carlyle had implied about Victoria.

The bulk of his anger lay with Miss Love. Had she not schemed to steal away with Mr. Ramsey, Victoria would not have been put in a position with Mr. Carlyle which was awkward enough for her to say anything as shocking as what Carlyle had implied she had said about seductions. Victoria did not say shocking things to anyone but him – and then, it was only because he had pushed her to the point of doing so.

Added to that sin was the abominable way in which Miss Love had treated Everett – and her sister. He glanced sideways at Grace. How could an older sister take advantage of a younger sister in such a fashion? Was Miss Love completely incapable of loving anyone save herself? He was about to inquire of Grace how she could abide such a sister when they were approached by Mrs. Love.

"Have you seen Felicity? Is she well? Why did you not tell me your sister was injured?" she demanded of Grace all in one breath.

"That is likely because she is not injured," Roger replied.

"But I have received a report that she is!"

"She did turn her ankle, but she said that it was nothing and that I was not to worry you about it," Grace said.

"She was not favouring either ankle when we saw her just now. However, her hair was a bit disheveled, and her cheeks looked rather pleasingly pink, which I would assume was due to the few stolen moments with Mr. Ramsey and not any particular injury."

Mrs. Love's eyes grew wide, and she turned once again to her youngest daughter. "Did you know your sister was planning to sneak off?"

Grace shook her head. "Not completely."

"What do you mean not completely? Either you did or you did not?"

"I knew it was likely and that it was what she wished." Grace's head dipped.

"Then, you did know."

"Yes," Grace whispered, "I knew all too well when she sent me back with Mr. Clayton. Until then, I was not entirely sure."

"Mr. Clayton is not with her?"

"No, he has given up on her," Roger said, "as any sensible fellow should."

Mrs. Love gasped.

"She has treated him very ill, madame."

"Has she indeed?"

She was questioning the fact? How could she not see that it was true beyond a shadow of a doubt?

"She ignored him while flirting with others and this after spending some stolen moments with him in the garden at Stratsbury Park." He motioned toward the rotunda. "And tonight, she has schemed to do the same thing with Mr. Ramsey without taking care whatsoever to hide it from Clayton, who is not happy about being rid of her at the moment, but he will be."

"Can all this be true?" She looked as if she was about to faint dead away.

"Yes, Mother," Grace answered.

"And you have helped her conceal this?"

"She asked me to."

"With all due respect, madame," Roger interrupted, for he did not wish to stand here discussing Grace's role in all of this when he needed to find Victoria, "I believe it is your eldest daughter who deserves your ire at present. I will return Miss Grace to the house."

Mrs. Love tipped her head and gave him a questioning look. "I have not seen you all day, and now you are here with my daughter. Why is that?"

Roger blew out a breath, but before he could say anything, Grace replied for him.

"He was looking for Miss Hamilton. He has only just arrived back from...where were you?"

"I went home."

"He has only just arrived back from his home and needs to speak to Miss Hamilton most urgently. So, I was helping him find her."

"We were never outside the view of the house, madame."

"Nothing untoward happened?"

"I would never treat your daughter so ill. Nor would she allow it."

"I would not?" Grace asked.

"No, do you not remember what you told me earlier when we were discussing Mr. Clayton?"

"Oh! Right!" She shook her head as she looked at her mother. "Mrs. Berkley told me that Mr. Shelton would never be tricked into marrying anyone. He would leave them ruined – not that he would ruin them, that part would be done by the lady's scheming – rather than be forced into marriage. And I would not be foolish enough to be ruined."

Mrs. Love wore a perplexed expression. "I think that is good?"

"Most admirable," Roger assured her. "Now, if I could return Grace to the house and find Miss Hamilton."

"Yes, yes," Mrs. Love still wore a bewildered expression. "She is in the house, and, from what I heard before Mrs. Berkley found me, Miss Hamilton was seen to be on her way upstairs with Mr. Clayton."

Had the woman said what he thought she had said?

"Why was she on her way upstairs with Mr. Clayton?" Grace asked.

Mrs. Love shook her head. "How should I know? However, it does seem rather improper."

It most certainly did! Roger gave Grace's arm a tug. "I think we should walk rapidly."

"If it would not cause a stir, I would suggest we run," Grace said as she scampered to keep up with him. "In fact, if you wish to run, I can find my way back to the house on my own."

"No, I told your mother I would see you there. I am a man of my word."

"For a gentleman with your reputation, Mr. Shelton, you are most shockingly noble."

Roger chuckled and thanked her. He had never taken advantage where advantage was not given. He was not a swindler – not even when it came to kisses. And while he had enjoyed every garden and alcove interlude of which he had been a part, and he was not opposed to presenting the suggestion of impropriety, not once had he stolen anything. However, all of that was in the past. Presently, he had only to find Victoria and persuade her to marry him and make him the happiest of all men.

"You!"

Roger stopped just inside the door to the drawing room as a red-faced gentleman approached him.

"May I be of service?" he asked warily. He had not seen Mr. Upton at the house party before this, but he knew him from town. The man was a rash, hot-headed man.

"Roger!"

He turned to see his sister hurrying toward him. It seemed he was not destined to make a quick and quiet entry.

"Where have you been?" Diana asked.

"With my sister," Mr. Upton said just before his fist made contact with Roger's chin.

Chapter 14

Roger staggered backward, rubbing his throbbing chin. "I went home," he said to Diana.

"Home?" Mr. Upton scoffed. "Not according to my sister."

"I swear I have not been with your sister," Roger said, dodging another punch before dropping his shoulder and charging the man, sending them both to the floor.

"You'll marry her!" Mr. Upton struggled to toss Roger off of him.

"I will not marry a liar." Roger sat on Mr. Upton and held the fellow's wrists. "And if your sister is the one who has told you that she was with me, she is most certainly a liar. I was at home. You can verify that with my mother, my father, and Mr. Berkley, as well as his infant son."

"Get off me!"

"Not unless you give me your word that you will not attack me again."

Mr. Upton struggled for a moment longer before assuring Roger that he would not hit him.

"Now," Roger said after he had risen, straightened his jacket, and smoothed his hair, "might we find a place to discuss this in a more gentlemanly fashion?" He rubbed his chin. A cold compress would be most welcome.

"The library," Mr. Upton suggested.

"A proper choice." Roger turned toward the door. "And bring your sister," he called over his shoulder.

"I would also like to speak to you." Diana followed him from the room. "However, I must go up to my charge and tell her that someone has spread a vicious rumor about her and Mr. Clayton."

Roger shook his head. "Vicious rumors seem to be the thing this evening."

Diana raised an eyebrow at him and scowled. "And if you had been here instead of dashing home, none of them would have started."

Her words smarted nearly as much as his chin. "I had a good reason to be gone." He caught her elbow before she could make her escape. "I spoke to your husband."

"About what?"

"Your hopes for me."

She tipped her head, her brow furrowing.

He blew out a slow breath as Mr. and Miss Upton joined them. "I will tell you more later. Just know that I wish for the same." He released his sister's elbow and motioned to the library. "After you."

"Diana," he called to his sister before he followed the Uptons into the library.

She turned toward him.

"I'm sorry."

She stood looking expectantly at him.

"For making a mess of things."

She smiled at him.

"You will tell Victoria that?"

She nodded.

"She is not with Clayton?"

Diana sighed and walked back to him. "It is a rumour. She is in her room. She fell – I believe while trying to avoid Mr. Carlyle."

Carlyle had caused harm to come to Victoria? Could fury cause a gentleman's heart to explode from beating too rapidly? He rubbed his chest. He was likely to discover the answer. "I should have injured him when I had the chance!"

Diana patted his cheek. "Later, dear. You have people waiting for you." She tipped her head toward the open door in front of which he stood.

He gave her a small smile and then, drawing a breath, joined the Uptons and a sleepy Yardley in the library where he crossed to the decanter of port and poured a small amount into a glass.

"Yardley, I am disappointed. You have not emptied this carafe."

"There is only so much one man can consume. Clayton did a fine job helping me consume that much." He glanced at their companions. "Should I leave?"

Roger shook his head. "There is no need. In fact, you might find this entertaining, and I would appreciate a witness should Mr. Upton decide to accost me again." Roger rubbed his chin.

"You hit Shelton?" Yardley asked Upton.

"He has ruined my sister." Upton stood behind the chair in which his sister sat.

"He has?" Yardley asked in surprise.

"No, he has not," Miss Upton protested.

"But I heard you say he," Upton stabbed the air in Roger's direction, "stole away to be with you."

Miss Upton's look of mortification deepened. Roger was confident that if the chair were to burst into flames and consume the young lady with it, she would not be coming back as a disgruntled ghost except perhaps to torment her brother.

"You did not hear everything." Her voice was barely above a whisper.

"I heard enough."

"No!" Miss Upton sprang from her chair and turned on her brother. "You never hear enough. You only ever hear what you wish, and you never stop to consider or verify if what you have heard is true."

"I... I... I... I do," Upton sputtered.

"No, you do not. Do you know how many per-fectly acceptable gentlemen have not called on me because you have heard something and assumed the worst? And now this! Why are you even here? Was not our aunt a good enough chaperone? Were you afraid I might actually make a match before you could ruin it?"

Roger leaned against the sideboard and nursed

his glass of port while watching the Uptons with interest.

"I am ruined!" Miss Upton dropped back into her chair and covered her face with her hands, her shoulders rising and falling in shuddering silent sobs.

"Why are you here?" Yardley asked Miss Upton's brother.

"Grandmother has taken ill and is not expected to survive the week."

Miss Upton gasped, and her sobs became audible. Roger's heart clenched at the plight of the young woman.

"I have been sent to see that all is well in here," Mr. Abernathy said as he entered the library. "My wife was fearful that one object or another might be injured in your discussion." He gave Roger a quizzical look with a tip of his head toward Miss Upton.

"Her grandmother is gravely ill," Roger replied. "And her brother is an idiot."

"I am sorry to hear it," Mr. Abernathy said. "Will you need to take your sister home?"

"Yes, sir," Mr. Upton answered. "I fear that my

mind is not right at the moment. It seems I heard something which was not what was said."

"Distressing circumstances can cause such to happen. Might I inquire what you heard that was not right?" Mr. Abernathy asked.

"My sister was speaking with your daughter when I arrived, and I heard my sister say that Shelton had stolen away to be with her." He shrugged. "I do not know what the rest was about. I apologize for arriving at a conclusion without all the facts. To both of you," he said, turning to look at Roger. "You would not consider marrying my sister, would you?"

Roger shook his head. "I am afraid I would not. Not that there is any particular deficit with your sister."

"Miss Upton," Mr. Abernathy said, "are you able to tell me about what you and my daughter were speaking which led to this unfortunate misunderstanding?"

"Miss... Love," she managed between sobs.

"What about Miss Love?" Mr. Abernathy pressed.

Miss Upton drew and released a breath as she

dried her cheeks with the handkerchief her brother had given her.

"We... had heard... a rumor that she had set her cap at... Mr. Ramsey." Her eyes were fixed on the handkerchief as she now twisted it in her hands as she gained control of her emotions. "He is very handsome and has a good fortune, unlike Mr. Clayton, who is only handsome and possesses a moderate fortune. Well, you see." She paused. "She had told Miss Abernathy 'I wish he would be like Mr. Shelton and steal away to be with me all day.' I was shocked, of course, and gasped just as my aunt joined us and made me repeat it to her." She sighed. "Which was just as my brother appeared."

"And decided to seek me out," Roger said.

Miss Upton nodded her head. "But I did not know that is what he was doing until he charged across the room at you. Can you forgive me?"

"Of course. As long as we do not have to marry," he replied with a wink.

She smiled.

"Was that the extent of my daughter's gossip?" Mr. Abernathy did not sound at all pleased.

Miss Upton nodded. "The only other thing that

was said before Mr. Shelton entered the drawing room was said by my aunt. She told us that Miss Love would not be best pleased to hear that her offcast – meaning Mr. Clayton," she clarified, "was seen going upstairs with Miss Hamilton."

"Did she say where she heard that?" Roger asked.

"No, she did not. I am not even certain if she heard it or saw it. I was going to ask her, but my brother..."

Roger nodded his understanding. "Miss Hamilton is in her room with my sister. She is not with Mr. Clayton. However, I heard the same thing from a different source."

Mr. Abernathy shook his head. "This is a fine mess, is it not?"

"Indeed," Roger agreed.

"I am almost sorry I have spent the whole evening in the library," Yardley muttered.

"I will speak to both my daughter and my wife." Mr. Abernathy turned toward the door which was flung open before he reached it.

"You cannot marry her." Victoria with a robe wrapped tightly about her and her hair hanging down her back in a braid paid no attention to the others in the room or her chaperone who was attempting softly to tell her that she should return to her room.

"I am not going to," Roger said.

"He is not?" Victoria asked Miss Upton.

"I said I was not." Roger folded his arms and raised a brow at her.

"I was only double checking," Victoria argued. "Where have you been? It is not right to leave without telling your sister or your friends where you have gone."

"I was at home."

"That is what I said," Diana inserted.

"But why? Why would you leave without telling me?"

Roger glanced around the room. "Please get the details of this correct when you share it," he said to the others, "I am not unfamiliar with scandal, but Miss Hamilton is new to it."

He took her hand and pulled her a step closer to him. "I went home to think. Mr. Brown sends his greetings."

"You went to the pond?"

He nodded. "I had something to consider. Recently, it had been pointed out to me that there was a lady in attendance at this house party who would make a very good match for me."

Her brow furrowed. "Why was she a good match?"

"Yes," Diana inserted, "I, too, would like to know that."

Roger glared at his sister briefly before turning his attention back to Victoria. Diana knew perfectly well why. The broad grin she wore confirmed it.

"You choose to ask why and not who?"

"I will ask who after you have told me why," Victoria retorted. "It is not polite to question how I question."

He chuckled. Even here when things were higgledy-piggledy, she scolded him. There had never been any pretense between them.

"Very well. Then, I shall answer why. She is a good match because I love her, most dearly."

Victoria's eyes grew wide. "Who?" Her whisper seemed to take a great deal of effort.

"You, my darling friend, you."

"Oh." She glanced around. "I think I require a chair."

"I'll not let you fall," Roger assured her, pulling

her into his embrace. "Unless, of course, you refuse me. Then, I shall let you gracefully drop to the floor."

She laughed. "Refuse you? What am I to refuse?"

"My offer of marriage."

"And why would I do that? I have loved you for years."

"But what about your reason for not marrying?" he teased.

She shook her head. "It is no longer a reason. For it was only a lack of an offer from you which kept me from marrying. But what about your reason?"

He squeezed her more tightly. "What is there to fear if my best, most beloved friend is my wife? I would rather lose anything other than you."

Her smile in response was all the answer he needed, but just to clarify for their audience, he asked, "You will marry me then?"

"Gladly. Most happily. With pleasure."

"You found her!" Grace cried from the door to the library, causing them both to turn toward her. "I was looking for you, Miss Hamilton, to tell you that Mr. Shelton was looking for you."

"She found me," Roger answered. "And has

saved me from a miserable life without her by accepting my offer."

Grace clapped her hands. "I had hoped so since you are holding her most improperly."

Victoria laughed along with Roger.

"We really do need to see her well-matched," Roger whispered to Victoria.

"Indeed, we do," Victoria replied.

"But not before we cause a bit of a stir." He gave her his best wolfish grin.

"And how shall we do that?"

"I think it must begin with a kiss." He bent his head to touch her lips with his. Then, he pulled back just a nose's-breath, and whispered, "I love you." After which, as any good rogue would, he claimed her lips once again in a deep, passionate kiss that sent shivers of delight through him and, to his great satisfaction, caused her to melt into his embrace and twine her fingers in his hair.

At that moment, he knew that his future would be perfect, not because there would never be any struggles or heartache, but because Victoria would be at his side both as his wife and his dearest, darling friend.

Before You Go

If you enjoyed this book, be sure to let others know by leaving a review.

~*~*~

Want to know when the next book in this series will be available?

You can always know what's new with my books by subscribing to my mailing list.

(There will, of course, be a thank you gift for joining because I think my readers are awesome!)

Book News from Leenie Brown

(bit.ly/LeenieBBookNews)

~*~*~

Turn the page to read an excerpt of another one of Leenie's books

Other Pens, Mansfield Park Excerpt

[Have you ever wondered what happened to Henry Crawford after *Mansfield Park* ended? How about his sister or Tom Bertram? What about his friends who were never at Mansfield Park? If you have wondered about such things, you'll want to read my *Other Pens, Mansfield Park* series, which mixes Jane Austen's classic characters with a cast of original ones in situations never found in one of Miss Austen's novels. Below is an excerpt from the second book in the series, *Charles: To Discover His Purpose*, a story about how Henry Crawford's rakish friend Charles Edwards find his happily ever after while attempting to steal a kiss.]

CHAPTER 1

Charles Edwards squinted into the late afternoon

sun – it was an action that he could almost do without any discomfort. The swelling around his eye had subsided, and soon, the bruising would fade to a nasty yellow and then disappear. Until that happened, he would continue to take his rides by wandering from one street to the next rather than face the taunting and questioning looks he was guaranteed to receive in the parks.

While it was an excellent way to avoid censure from his peers, it was dashed boring trotting up and down streets without so much as a single friend with whom to converse. Had he earned his scars more gallantly, perhaps he would not feel the need to hide them. To have been injured in a boxing match or defense of some lady's honor would make his bruises more of a badge than a blemish. However, since everyone in town had likely read that blasted article in the paper, the raised eyebrows from overprotective matrons and giggles from their charges would be unbearable. And then, there would be the gentlemen. He shook his head. Had he received a blackened eye from Trefor Linton for actually doing something inappropriate with Linton's sister, Constance, his friends would just laugh and clap him on the shoulder before filling his glass with some libation at his club.

But, he had not been caught doing anything improper. In fact, it was much worse than just not being found dallying with a debutante. He had been attempting to be gallant. He would do his best not to be put in such a situation again! Honourable actions and favours to ladies who were offering none in return must be avoided, for they only led to broken noses, disgrace, and lonely rambles up less well-to-do streets.

"Mr. Edwards?"

Charles drew his horse to a stop just in front of a carriage that was standing at the ready to receive a lovely young woman. He had not bothered to take note of her since this was not the part of town where the finest flowers of the season resided.

"Miss Linton," he said doffing his hat. "Is Crawford with you?" He nodded to the carriage.

"No," Constance Linton replied with a smile, "though he very much wanted to be. It is just Evelyn and I."

His brows furrowed. Evelyn? The name sounded familiar.

"Miss Barrett," Constance clarified.

"Ah, Miss Barrett. Of course. How negligent of me to not remember." How had he managed to forget her name? He certainly had not forgotten her perfectly pink lips or lithe figure...the same figure that was exiting the house to his left. She was perhaps the most enticing creature he had ever met and never sampled.

"Oh!"

Miss Barrett's lips formed such a wonderfully kissable *o*.

"Mr. Edwards," she greeted with a small curtsey. "Are you here to visit Mrs. Verity and the children?"

His brows furrowed again. "Mrs. Who?"

"Verity," Evelyn repeated. "She runs this home for children." She motioned toward the house.

"I did not know this was a home for children." His left brow rose in question. "Why are you here? None of these children are yours, I would assume."

Her eyes grew wide, and she gasped. "We are not all as reprobate as you, Mr. Edwards."

He leaned forward, nonchalantly admiring her look of utter indignation. "Then, what, pray tell, are proper young ladies such as yourself and Miss Linton doing here?"

"Charitable work. You do know what that is, do you not?"

He chuckled. Miss Barret was not the sort to shy away quietly to her corner and leave him be. He liked that. "I have heard the term."

"But have you ever experienced it?" asked Constance.

He shifted his gaze to his friend, Henry Crawford's, betrothed. "No, not beyond what is expected on my father's estate."

"It's rather fulfilling," Constance replied. "Today, we taught some children their letters. It was remarkable, was it not, Evelyn?" She wore a look of sheer delight.

"And Linton approves of this?" Charles asked.

"Both he and Henry do."

Delight did not begin to describe the look in Miss Linton's eyes as she said the name Henry. One day, when he was ready to take up his mantle of responsibility, Charles hoped to find a lady who would look even half as happy saying his name as Miss Linton did at this moment.

"Trefor," Constance continued, "thought this would be a safe way to keep me occupied. My last scheme, you see, did not leave him favourably disposed to allowing me to find ways in which to make my life more interesting."

There was a mischievous gleam in both her eyes and those of her friend Evelyn. Curious, that. He had not expected anything akin to impishness from Trefor Linton's sister or any of her friends. Constance Linton was the most proper chit he had ever met, and he suspected, to be her friend, Miss Barrett must be the same.

"Is your eye feeling better?" Miss Barrett asked.

"It is, but I'll not be doing either of you any favours in the future," he replied with a smirk. "At least not unless I receive something better than a broken nose and a black eye in return."

"I can neither apologize or thank you enough," Constance replied.

She had apologized over and over and over again as she stood holding a compress to his eye in the Linton sitting room those many days ago. "I think you have said the words enough," he replied softly. "I merely jest." He would not have her feeling guilty for his injuries when it was not her doing which caused them.

Miss Barrett tipped her head as she looked up at him, a puzzled look on her face. Then, she shook herself and smiled. "We are expected at your house soon, Connie. Mother will be waiting."

"As will Trefor," she smiled, "and Henry."

Much to Charles's surprise, Miss Evelyn Barrett rolled her eyes at the tone her friend used to say Henry's name.

"Do not let me detain you. I would not wish to run afoul of any of them." He winked at Miss Barret. "At least, not until I am healed."

She gasped. "My mother has warned me about you, Mr. Edwards."

"As well she should," he replied easily. "I am dreadfully charming."

Constance had entered the carriage, but Evelyn, who remained on the street, laughed. "That is not how my mother said it." Her eyes sparkled with impertinence. Then, with a small curtsey of parting, she boarded her carriage.

Charles looked after her and tipped his hat as the door closed on those shining eyes and teasing smile. Oh, he could find great pleasure in evoking such a look from her on a regular basis. Not that he wished to spend great amounts of time with her. No, he was not the sort of gentleman to trot around behind a lady hoping for her to smile at him or laugh at his jokes. He danced; he flirted; and he stole kisses. He did not become attached. Attachments were dangerous. They led to marriage and, he fought the urge to shudder, responsibility. He was far too young for such things as that just yet.

Still, he wondered where she would be this evening and if there would be any dark corners into which she might be persuaded.

He blew out a breath. Hiding himself away from society was perhaps not the best idea in the world. It apparently was wreaking havoc on his well-ordered, carefree existence. A rogue such as himself did not stalk his prey. He simply looked for the opportunity and took it. Planning anything was far too much like being responsible. Rules, guidelines, ledgers, accounts, and all the rest that went with being a gentleman of standing belonged to his father, not Charles.

In front of him, the carriage stopped, a man jumped down, the door opened, and a pretty face peered out, looking back to where he was.

He nudged his horse forward as Miss Barrett waved him towards her.

"Do you require help?" he asked as he drew near.

"No, no, we are well. Connie and I were just

talking, and I thought as we were discussing how dreadful it is that you were injured on Connie's account that it would be charitable of us to offer you a place in the Linton's box at the theatre tonight."

Charles began to shake his head.

"Hear me out. Do not refuse until I have made my full request. And come forward more, I feel as if I am going to fall out of this door and onto the street."

Charles chuckled. This young woman sounded more like Linton's cantankerous Aunt Gwladys than a young lady of the ton. Most young ladies who presented themselves during the season went out of their way to appear demure to one and all – always.

"Do you scold everyone?" he teased as he did as she said.

If he had expected her to be offended, he was once again going to be surprised, for she merely smiled, batted her lashes, and replied, "No, I scold very few beyond my brother actually."

"So, I am special," he returned.

She shrugged. "Perhaps you are. Or perhaps I just find you as troublesome as Griffin."

"I think I will insist you find me special."

"Do what you will; it matters not one jot to me," she retorted.

Her words might have said she did not care, but her tone clearly said she was annoyed.

"As I was saying…"

"Before you began scolding." Charles smiled at her huff.

"Before I had to pause to give instructions."

Charles chuckled. "Continue. I shall not refuse until you have said your piece."

"Refuse? You intend to refuse?"

"Most likely. But, I have not heard your request in full, so I cannot be certain I am correct until I do. I have been wrong before."

Her brows rose, and her lips pursed for a moment as if she were holding back some retort.

"There will not be very many people in our box. If you slip in a side door or something and scurry up to the box, you will not have to have many people gawk at you."

"You think I am worried about being seen?"

"I would be if my eye were the colour of yours. That *is* why you are riding here and not in a more populated place, is it not? And, I have not seen you at any events since...well..." she pointed to her eye.

"I will admit that I do not relish the whispers." Why he felt he needed to admit such a thing was beyond him. He could come up with any number of reasons to be riding where he was and for not having been at any soiree she had attended. A smile slipped slowly across his face. "Have you missed me?"

"What?" She shook her head vigorously. "No. I just noticed that I had not seen you slinking from shadow to shadow."

"If you say so."

"I do." She scowled. "Now, will you be joining us? I am certain no one would be in the least put out if you did."

"How reassuring," Charles muttered.

"Please," Constance added from the interior of the carriage. "I do feel dreadful that you have been out of society. It must be terribly boring sitting at home instead of going out."

"Who said I was sitting at home?" He smiled a lazy, suggestive smile.

"Henry," Constance replied.

Blast! Did Henry tell her everything?

"Very well, I have been hiding away. Are you happy to know my shame?"

"Only if it means you will join us," said Miss Barrett.

"Can you not muster an ounce of sympathy?" he asked in surprise. Were not young ladies – especially those who did charity work – supposed to be compassionate?

She shook her head. "No. Not a morsel. While I am awfully sorry you were injured, I do believe you have escaped more times than you have been caught."

The lady might look like an angel, but she had a heart of ice. However, ice could be melted. In fact, it could be quite a marvelous lark to attempt to melt that ice.

"Very well, I will join you if you will but attempt to feel an ounce of pity for me."

The way her lips pursed with contained amusement was tempting. "A full ounce?"

"Yes." He moved closer to her door. "A full ounce." He repeated the words in a low, sultry tone – slowly and deliberately. Satisfaction curled his lips as he saw her pretty nibble-worthy neck rise and fall when she swallowed.

She licked her lips. "I shall make an attempt."

"Then, I shall see you at the theatre."

"Very good."

He chuckled at the uncertainty in her voice. Again, he tipped his hat to the closed carriage door and watched it drive away before continuing on his way home to prepare for an evening of entertainment – and a play.

Acknowledgements

There are many who have had a part in the creation of this story. Some have read and commented on it. Some have proofread for grammatical errors and plot holes. Others have not even read the story and a few, I know, will never read it. However, their encouragement and belief in my ability, as well as their patience when I became cranky or when supper was late or the groceries ran low, was invaluable.

And so, I would like to say *thank you* to Zoe, Rose, Kristine, Ben, and Kyle. I feel blessed through your help, support, and understanding.

I have not listed my dear husband in the above group because, to me, he deserves his own special thank you, for, without his somewhat pushy insistence that I start sharing my writing, none of my writing goals and dreams would have been met.

Other Leenie B Books

You can find all of Leenie's books at this link
bit.ly/LeenieBBooks
where you can explore the collections below

~*~

Other Pens, Mansfield Park

~*~

Touches of Austen Collection

~*~

Other Pens, Pride and Prejudice

~*~

Dash of Darcy and Companions Collection

~*~

Marrying Elizabeth Series

~*~

Willow Hall Romances

~*~

The Choices Series

~*~

Darcy Family Holidays

~*~

Darcy and... An Austen-Inspired Collection

About the Author

Leenie Brown has always been a girl with an active imagination, which, while growing up, was both an asset, providing many hours of fun as she played out stories, and a liability, when her older sister and aunt would tell her frightening tales. At one time, they had her convinced Dracula lived in the trunk at the end of the bed she slept in when visiting her grandparents!

Although it has been years since she cowered in her bed in her grandparents' basement, she still has an imagination which occasionally runs away with her, and she feeds it now as she did then — by reading!

Her heroes, when growing up, were authors, and the worlds they painted with words were (and still are) her favourite playgrounds! Now, as an adult, she spends much of her time in the Regency world, playing with the characters from her favourite Jane Austen novels and those of her own creation.

When she is not traipsing down a trail in an attempt to keep up with her imagination, Leenie resides in the beautiful province of Nova Scotia with her two sons and her very own Mr. Brown (a wonderful mix of all the best of Darcy, Bingley, and Edmund with a healthy dose of the teasing Mr. Tilney and just a dash of the scolding Mr. Knightley).

Connect with Leenie

E-mail:

LeenieBrownAuthor@gmail.com

Facebook:

www.facebook.com/LeenieBrownAuthor

Blog:

leeniebrown.com

Patreon:

https://www.patreon.com/LeenieBrown

Subscribe to Leenie's Mailing List:

Book News from Leenie Brown

(bit.ly/LeenieBBookNews)